"He *Kissed* You? An Honest To God Knee-melting Kiss?"

Pru nodded. "Then he warned me not to get any ideas about him."

"And are you?" Laura asked, grinning.

"I'm going to marry him," she announced, then sat back and waited for the explosion. It didn't take long.

"You're going to *what?*"

"I'm going to marry—"

"I heard that part!" Laura exclaimed. "Lord, when you were talking about this yesterday, I didn't realize you meant the big M. How can you be thinking about marrying the guy when you don't even know him? You've spent one evening with him. One evening!"

"I know," Pru agreed. "It sounds crazy, doesn't it? I can't explain it. I just know every time I look in Zebadiah Murdock's eyes, I know I'm going to marry him. Now all I have to do is convince *him*."

Dear Reader,

As always, I am proud to be bringing you the very best that romance has to offer—starting with an absolutely wonderful *Man of the Month* from Annette Broadrick called *Mysterious Mountain Man*. A book from Annette is always a real treat, and I know this story—her fortieth for Silhouette—will satisfy her fans and gain her new ones!

As readers, you've told me that you *love* miniseries, and you'll find some of the best series right here at Silhouette Desire. This month we have *The Cop and the Chorus Girl*, the second book in Nancy Martin's delightful *Opposites Attract* series, and *Dream Wedding*, the next book in Pamela Macaluso's *Just Married* series.

For those who like a touch of the supernatural, look for Linda Turner's *Heaven Can't Wait*. Lass Small's many fans will be excited about her latest, *Impulse*. And Kelly Jamison brings us a tender tale about a woman who returns to her hometown to confront her child's father in *Forsaken Father*.

Don't miss any of these great love stories!

Lucia Macro,
Senior Editor

Please address questions and book requests to:
Silhouette Reader Service
U.S.: 3010 Walden Ave., P.O. Box 1325, Buffalo, NY 14269
Canadian: P.O. Box 609, Fort Erie, Ont. L2A 5X3

LINDA TURNER
HEAVEN CAN'T WAIT

SILHOUETTE *Desire*
Published by Silhouette Books
America's Publisher of Contemporary Romance

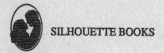 SILHOUETTE BOOKS

ISBN 0-373-05929-9

HEAVEN CAN'T WAIT

Copyright © 1995 by Linda Turner

Books by Linda Turner

LINDA TURNER

began reading romances in high school and began writing them one night when she had nothing else to read. She's been writing ever since. Single and living in Texas, she travels every chance she gets, scouting locales for her books.

SPECIAL THANKS

To my Great Uncle George Dawson, who really is a great uncle. Thanks for letting me pick your brain about construction. You'll never know how much you helped me. Hopefully, I didn't make too many mistakes.

And to Barbara Catlin for the title. It's perfect.

Prologue

───

They stood hand in hand, two lovers who had withstood the test of time, the love they shared for each other setting their hearts and auras aglow with a golden light that could be seen in the outermost realms of Heaven. Staring down at them, his own affection for them making it impossible for him to be stern, St. Peter struggled to hold back a smile. He didn't usually handle the problems of ordinary souls, but these were two of his favorites and they obviously needed his help. "What am I going to do with you two? You blew it again."

"It was my fault. I had no idea when I took that earlier train to New York in 1901 that I would miss my one and only chance to meet her—"

"No, I was ready," she quickly cut in, giving his fingers a squeeze. "*I* should have left for the station instead of waiting for the weather to clear. But I was worried about ruining my new shoes, and by the time I boarded the next train, he was already gone."

So they had missed each other. Again.

Flipping through their joint file, St. Peter studied the recorded images that moved before him like a motion picture. They'd spent numerous lifetimes together on earth, lifetimes when they should have met and fallen in love, then spent valuable years together learning necessary lessons that could only be mastered in the physical realm. But in Medieval England, before their paths had ever had a chance to cross, he had left for the Crusades and died before his time on the hot, dry sands of Arabia. Then there was the middle of the nineteenth century. Everything should have worked out perfectly then. They were both headed for the California gold-fields, where they should have come face to face in the ungodly little town of Black Bear Gulch in the Cascades. Instead she had never made it to California because she had left the wagon train in Kansas to become a teacher in a backwater community that no one but God had ever heard of.

In each incarnation, having missed their one true love, they had each gone through their lifetimes unmarried, choosing to be alone and lonely rather than mated to someone else. Considering that, it wasn't surprising that neither had lived very long in lifetime after lifetime.

It was, St. Peter decided, frustrating enough to make an angel second class despair of ever earning his wings.

"This cannot continue, dear hearts," he told them with a frown. "You must know that. There are things you need to learn and experience, and if you can't find each other on earth, then you have to find someone else."

"No!"

They cried out in unison, staring at him in horror as if he had just suggested they stab each other in the back. Wincing, St. Peter sighed in defeat. He'd never seen two soul mates more devoted to each other, more loyal to a love that showed every sign of lasting an eternity. But if they were ever going to get together on earth, it was obvious they were going to need some help.

That's against the rules, Peter. The most important lesson a soul learns on earth is the consequences of free choice.

The voice that echoed in his head was kind and loving and gently reproving. Under normal circumstances, Peter would have obeyed it in a heartbeat. But the two unhappy souls standing so pitifully before him gave strong testimony to the belief that some rules were meant to be bent.

Taking a chance and praying he wasn't making a mistake, Peter told his two charges, "I'm going to give you another chance, but this time I'm going to personally see that your paths cross. And to make sure that nothing goes wrong, one of you will recognize the other as the love of your life the second your eyes meet."

"Who—"

"You'll find out soon enough," he continued. "And it will be that soul's task to convince the other that you were made for each other. It won't be easy," he warned when they started to smile. "You will be different ages and have numerous obstacles thrown in your path. But true love is worth fighting for and you can't let anything get in your way."

"Oh, we won't. We won't."

"We promise."

Reaching out to place a big strong hand on each of their shoulders, he smiled down at them lovingly. "I have all the faith in the heavens in you. Now go. You've got a journey to prepare for."

In the blink of an eye, they were gone, so excited their feet hardly touched the clouds. Staring after them, St. Peter's smile turned rueful. They were all taken care of. Now all he had to do was square his plans with the big guy.

Peter, what have you done?

"Nothing too radical, Lord," he said hastily. "I admit I bent the rules a little, but only because I know how strongly you feel about true love." Behind his back, he crossed his fingers. "Trust me. Everything's going to work out fine." He hoped.

One

<hr>

Something wasn't right.

Her eyes on her feet, Prudence Sullivan took a slow turn across the concrete floor of the east wing of what was to be the Fifth Army's new state-of-the-art communications center at Fort Sam Houston in San Antonio. As a substitute for Eric Thompson, the government inspector normally assigned to the construction site, she wasn't expected to do much except make sure nothing went wrong while Eric was on sick leave. She certainly wasn't supposed to concern herself with a floor that had been approved weeks ago. But a familiar knotting in her gut warned her a mistake had been made somewhere. A mistake it was her job to catch.

Not liking her suspicions, she squatted to run her hand over the bare concrete. It felt fine, but she knew from experience that that didn't mean diddly. If an unscrupulous contractor wanted to save some money and cheat on the specs, he could make a concrete floor that wouldn't hold office furniture without cracking look like a work of art.

Still balanced on her haunches, she pushed her hard hat to the back of her head and frowned up at Roy Wilkins, the field superintendent. A bear of a man, he cast a shadow that would have done an oak proud as he returned her frown with a wary one of his own. The big boss was gone for the day, and Roy had obviously been told not to let her out of his sight. He'd stuck to her side like glue from the moment she'd shown up at the site an hour ago.

Another time Pru would have been amused by his watch-dog hostility. She never understood why builders and contractors were so resentful of inspectors—she just made sure they did what they'd originally promised to do, which was put up a good building. But today, with the knots in her stomach drawing tight as a noose, she was anything but amused. "Who approved this floor?"

"Thompson."

Pru nodded, her green eyes shifting back to the concrete. She didn't know Eric personally, but that wasn't surprising. She was new to the job, new to the city, new to Texas. In fact, if she hadn't visited Laura, her college roommate and best friend, on Labor Day, she'd probably still be in Kansas City, where she'd been born and raised. But she'd taken one look at San Antonio and had instantly known that that was where she belonged.

Her family had thought she was crazy, of course, and she'd had to agree. But that hadn't stopped her from moving. And the moment she'd driven into the city with everything she owned packed in the U-Haul trailer attached to her Jeep, she'd felt like she was coming home.

It was almost as if the powers that be were lighting her path, she'd thought whimsically. She'd stepped right from her old job as a city inspector into one with the government. She'd started two weeks ago and loved the work, even though it didn't give her much of a chance to meet other inspectors. When she was on the job, the man she was replacing wasn't.

Which meant she didn't know a damn thing about Eric Thompson. He could be conscientious and dedicated...or an unethical jackass who took money on the side to look the other way when something wasn't up to code. Torn, she pushed to her feet. She hated to doubt another inspector, but the feel of the concrete under her feet gave her no choice.

"You're not going to like this—" she began, but before she could give Roy Wilkins the bad news, her beeper went off. One look at the number that flashed across the small screen and she swallowed a groan. Great. As if she didn't have enough problems, she now had to deal with her boss. Wonderful.

Bruce James didn't like her and probably never would. He'd resented her from the moment *his* supervisor had hired her...because she was a woman. A chauvinist right down to his shorts, he'd made no secret of the fact that he thought females had no business on a construction site and just as soon as he could find a way to send her packing, he would.

Wishing she could drop the beeper down the nearest open drain, she turned to Roy. "Is there a phone around here? I need to call my boss."

Seconds later she was seated at the desk in the small portable shed that served as the contractor's office, her voice coolly professional as she greeted her supervisor. "This is Pru, Mr. James. Is there a problem?"

"That's what you're getting paid to tell me, Sullivan," he retorted coldly. "How's the site?"

Later, Pru couldn't say what set the alarm bells clanging in her head, but something in his tone jarred her. He knew, she realized suddenly, astonished. Somehow, some way, he knew something was wrong at the site and he was just waiting to see if she was going to turn in one of her fellow inspectors or keep her mouth shut. If she did the former, her name would be mud with her cohorts; the latter, and she'd be fired so fast she wouldn't know what hit her.

The rat had set her up! she thought indignantly, clutching the phone as if it was his skinny neck. She could smell the stench from here. Wishing she had the financial independence to tell the jerk exactly what she thought of him, she asked sweetly, "What did you say Eric Thompson was out on sick leave for?"

"I didn't," he snapped. "Not that it's any of your business, but he fell on the site about a month ago and cracked his head. He's been having headaches ever since, so his doctor had him come in today for some tests."

"The fall...was it before or after the cement was poured?"

"Before, I believe. Why?"

"Then that would explain why he approved this spongy cement," she said, the triumph she couldn't quite conceal turning her voice the tiniest bit smug. "His brains were obviously scrambled and he wasn't thinking clearly. Don't worry, though, I'll take core samples just to make sure my instincts are right. Gotta go, boss. Talk to you later."

"Damn you, Sullivan, don't you hang up on me!"

Her dimpled grin full of mischief, Pru gently replaced the receiver in its cradle.

"You're not serious."

Lost in the satisfaction of the small victory, her eyes flew to the open doorway where Roy had appeared without her noticing. From his glare it was clear that he'd caught enough of the conversation not to like what he'd heard. "I'm afraid so," she said quietly, her smile fading. "I'm pretty sure Thompson made a mistake approving that cement. I'll need to see the results of the slump tests and the cylinders, but even if they're okay, I'm still going to take core samples. You can't pour any more, though, until the results come back from the lab. I'm sorry."

He cursed, her apology offering little consolation when he was all ready to start pouring the west wing. Each day she held up construction cost them not only time but money. "If you think I'm ticked, wait till you have to deal with Murdock," he warned. "He's going to be madder than a rooster with a bee up its butt."

An understatement of the grossest proportions. Zebadiah Murdock was, in fact, livid. "What the hell do you mean *work's been shut down!*" he barked into the phone an hour later. "By who?"

Wincing, Roy held the phone farther away from his ear. "Pru Sullivan," he said in disgust. "The new inspector who's substituting for Eric Thompson. She's being a real hard ass, boss. Going over everything with a fine-tooth comb, not giving an inch. She claims the concrete's not right in the east wing, so she's getting core samples. Until the test results come back, we can't pour squat."

"But Thompson already approved that!"

"I know," Roy grumbled. "But try telling her that. Once the lady makes up her mind, you can't move her with a forklift."

Murdock swore long and hard. He'd had nothing but problems with the Fort Sam project from the very beginning—delayed permits, bad weather, missing blueprints and tools—and now this. A lady inspector with a chip on her shoulder, looking to prove herself in a man's world by being hard as nails. Dammit, why *his* project? And why did this kind of crap have to hit when he was stuck in Austin testifying before a state committee? Trouble was brewing, and he was tied up with politicians who liked to hear themselves talk when he needed to be back in San Antonio.

"Put her on the line," he ordered.

He could practically hear Roy swallow. "Uh, do you think that's smart? You don't sound like you're in the best of moods and if you say something to get her back up, we ain't ever going to get anywhere on this job."

"Put her on, Roy. I want to talk to her."

When he spoke in that tone, people—especially his crew—listened. "Okay, but don't say I didn't warn you. Hang on and I'll get her."

Murdock waited impatiently, promising himself he wasn't going to lose his temper. He wasn't like a lot of the other builders he knew. He had no problem with women on a construction site...as long as they did their job just like everyone else and didn't get in his way.

"This is Pru Sullivan."

Her voice in his ear was low and husky and sexy as hell. Surprised, Murdock felt a heat he was unprepared for streak through him like summer lightning. Stunned, he almost dropped the phone. *This* was a government inspector?

"Hello? Is anyone there?"

The throaty query snapped him back to attention, bringing an uncomfortable flush to his cheeks. "This is Murdock," he said curtly. "The builder whose project you just shut down. You want to tell me what the hell you think you're doing, lady? I know you're just a sub, but you ought to check things out before you start throwing your weight around. That cement you've got a problem with has already passed inspection."

Well used to dealing with angry men, Pru refused to let him goad her into a sharp comeback. "My title is inspector, not 'lady,' Mr. Murdock, and I'd appreciate it if you'd remember that in the future," she said in a voice that was as cool as his was heated. "If you have a problem with that, then Pru or Ms. Sullivan will do. I don't answer to *lady.*"

"What I have a problem with," he said through his tightly clenched teeth, "is a woman who obviously doesn't know what she's doing and refuses to admit it. If you're not qualified to do the job, have the guts to say so and let James send over someone who is. In case you didn't know it, you're costing me money, *lady,* and I can't afford you."

For just a second the temper that went along with the red glints in her mahogany hair flashed in her eyes before she brought herself up short. No, she wasn't going to let the insufferable man get to her. After all, it wasn't as if she had to work with him on a regular basis. She just had to get through today, and he wasn't even on the site.

Cheered by the thought, her eyes started to dance. "Don't blame me for your own incompetency, Mr. Murdock," she said sweetly.

"Murdock," he growled. "It's just Murdock."

Willing to be gracious when she was about to win an argument, she said easily, "Okay, Murdock it is. You should have seen how thin that concrete was when it was poured, so if you want to blame someone, blame yourself. And, yes, it's true, Thompson did pass it. But he'd just suffered a blow to the head and couldn't have known what he was doing. If he'd have checked the results of the cylinder tests, he would have seen there was a problem."

"Thompson *was* the problem," he stressed. "When those cylinders were filled, he didn't handle them properly and everyone knew it. He had them rolling around like bowling balls in the back of his pickup, so don't talk to me about test results. They aren't worth the paper they're written on."

"Maybe not to you—"

"Dammit, there's nothing wrong with that cement!"

His angry roar startled Pru's heart into a crazy pounding and, unexpectedly, tugged up one corner of her mouth in a smile. Lord, the man had a short fuse! Did he think that just because he barked at her like a drill sergeant she would jump to attention and salute?

Grinning, she shrugged. "I wouldn't take any bets on that, Murdock. I know my onions...and my cement."

He'd have had to have been deaf to miss the laughter lacing her words, and he was a long way from that. "So you think this is amusing, do you? I—"

He broke off suddenly, cursing under his breath as a page announced that the committee was reconvening.

"I've got to go," he said shortly. "But don't make the mistake of thinking this conversation is over, *Inspector*. I don't lie or cheat or cut corners, and when I tell you that cement was poured according to specs, you can take it to the bank. But you go ahead and take your core samples and have them tested. When they come back, up to standard, I'm going to laugh in your face and have your job."

It wasn't an idle threat and they both knew it. She was holding up a government project worth millions of dollars solely because of a gut feeling that something was wrong. If she was right, she would have the satisfaction of throwing the truth in Zebadiah Murdock's face. If she was wrong, then Murdock wouldn't have to go after her. Her boss would beat him to the punch.

Standing at St. Peter's side, his assistant, Joshua, shook his head sadly as the two souls hung up, each muttering about the other. "They seem to have gotten off to a bad start, sir. And they haven't even met, yet. With Eric Thompson coming back in the morning, it looks like they never will."

"Oh, I don't know," St. Peter gently disagreed with a smile. "I think things are coming along nicely. And don't worry about tomorrow. I have a feeling that the wind is going to shift directions during the night, and you know what that means. Change is in the air. Watch."

When Pru reported to the office the next morning, it was only to get her next assignment and get out of there. If she could do that without having to once lay eyes on Bruce James, all the better. Luck, however, wasn't with her. The second she stepped through the door, her boss was there, almost as if he'd been waiting for her.

"I want to talk to you."

It wasn't, Pru decided, going to be her day. "If it's about yesterday," she began, "I've already taken the core samples—"

"I fired Eric Thompson this morning. The Fort Sam project is all yours."

Pru couldn't have been more surprised if he'd told her he was her Aunt Sally. Caught off guard, she just looked at him. He was lying. He had to be. As obnoxious as he was, even Bruce James wouldn't be so cold as to fire a man who'd made a mistake right after he'd been injured on the job. But one look at his ferretlike face told her not only would he, he had.

She *almost* told him then what a low-life, scumbag of a weasel he was, and damn the consequences. But the slight curve of his mouth was expectant, his beady black eyes bright with anticipation, and she knew that that was exactly what he wanted her to do. Then he would fire her for insubordination and direct her to the nearest unemployment line.

Oh, no, you don't. you little worm, she thought grimly, her expression carefully guarded under his watchful gaze. *You're not going to get rid of me that easily.* "Fine," she said indifferently. "I'll get right over there."

Judging from the way his already thin mouth squeezed into a flat line of annoyance, her reaction wasn't the one he'd been hoping for. But Pru could find little satisfaction in the triumph. Now instead of just working with one irritating man, she had to deal with two. And there was nothing funny about working with Zebadiah Murdock.

Heading for the site, she tried to tell herself it wasn't going to be that bad. She'd heard of Murdock long before she'd ever subbed for Eric Thompson, and what she'd heard, she'd liked. He'd started out as an ordinary carpenter, worked hard and learned fast, and gradually started his own small construction company. But with a talent for bringing projects in on schedule and under budget, he had become a success almost overnight. The Fort Sam project was his first with the government, but no one expected it to be his last.

In spite of the problems with the cement, he had a reputation for being honest and straight as an arrow. As the contractor, he could have spent his days doing paperwork in the air-conditioned comfort of his office, but Pru had learned from his men that he liked to work side by side with his crew in the hot sun. Evidently he hadn't forgotten his roots, and she liked that about him. But it was also common knowledge that he'd never met an inspector that he thought was worth a damn.

They'd probably be at each other's throats within an hour.

Common courtesy dictated that she immediately search him out and introduce herself as soon as she arrived at the site, but as she parked and plopped her hard hat on her head, she knew she wasn't going to do it. She hadn't forgotten their conversation of yesterday and she doubted that he had, either. She'd give him a little more time to cool off... and give herself a chance to adjust to the sudden change in her working conditions.

She learned from one of the plumbers that Murdock was handling a problem with one of the steel tiers in the west wing. Turning in the opposite direction, she intended to check the roughing-in the electricians were finishing at the other end of the building, but she'd only

taken two steps when the distinct sound of a cement
truck rolling onto the site stopped her in her tracks.
Whirling, she turned just in time to see the truck rumble over to the west wing, where men were already
waiting to spread the cement as it was poured.

Stunned that someone would dare to countermand
her order that there would be no more cement poured
until the results from the core sample came back, she
started to run. "Who ordered this cement? Stop right
this minute! Do you hear me? I said—"

Indignation blinding her to everything but the cement truck that was preparing to pour, she didn't even
see the man who cut across the compound with long
strides to intercept her until she all but slammed into
him. Staggering back a step, her breath escaped in a
gasp. "Oh, I'm sorry! I didn't see—"

The words died on her tongue, whatever she was going to say next lost forever as her gaze locked with the
most incredible blue eyes she'd ever seen. Her heart
pounding crazily in her chest and the cement truck forgotten, Pru stood dumbstruck, as dazed and disori-
ented as if she'd been run over by a train.

He was tall, a good six inches taller than her own five
foot ten, his body lean and hard and fat free in faded
jeans, a navy T-shirt and work boots. The yellow hard
hat he wore proclaimed him one of the crew, but even
without that giveaway, she would have known he was a
man who labored in the sun. His bronzed, weathered
skin was stretched tight across his chiseled face, the
crow's feet that mapped the corners of his eyes and
mouth a product of age and years spent working in the
elements.

With a touch of gray in the midnight black hair that
peaked out from underneath his hard hat, he could have

been anywhere between thirty-five and fifty, Pru acknowledged dazedly. But by no stretch of the imagination could he be considered old. Rugged, too roughly cut to ever pass for a polished diamond, he was the kind of man who could make a woman pant.

She knew him.

Recognition came out of nowhere, grabbing her by the heart, stunning her speechless. Oh, she didn't know his name and she would have bet she'd never seen him before—she would have remembered those eyes!—yet somehow she knew all she needed to know about him.

He was the one. The one she'd been waiting for. The one she'd moved from Kansas to San Antonio to find.

The absurdity of the thought nearly knocked her for a loop. *The one?* she echoed wildly. Good Lord, was she out of her mind? She hadn't moved to Texas to find anyone. She'd just been standing out in the sun too long.

Abruptly coming to her senses, she took a jerky step back, twin flags of hot color flying high in her cheeks. "Ex-excuse me," she said huskily. "I—I didn't s-see you."

She might not have noticed him, but Murdock had seen her the second she'd started running toward that damn cement truck with one hand flattened on her head to hold her hard hat in place. And he'd guessed immediately who she was. He hadn't been expecting her, but he would have known that velvety rough voice of hers in the bowels of hell.

So this was the hard-assed Prudence Sullivan, he thought irritably, surprised to find himself nearly eye to eye with her. His brows snapping together in a dark, intimidating line, he glared at her and realized too late that if the lady was hard-assed, you couldn't tell it from looking at her. Dammit, why hadn't anyone told him? Warned him? Dressed in khakis, she was tall and willowy, with her long, wavy, mahogany hair, caught up in a ponytail under her hard-hat, flashing fire in the sun. How she still managed to look soft and feminine in that getup, he'd be damned if he knew.

His gaze slowly sliding over her cream-like complexion, his jaw flexed in reaction. She had the old-fashioned, porcelain features of a china doll and a sweet, vulnerable mouth that a man dreamed of—and ached for—in the dead of night. And if she was a day out of her twenties, he'd eat his shorts.

Too young, he thought, taking a mental step back. He'd be forty-five next July, and he only had to look at the lady to feel like a lecher. Dammit, what was the government thinking of, assigning a woman like her to a building site full of rough, crude construction workers? Didn't those paper pushers know the hard hats would eat her up with a spoon if given half the chance?

Disgusted with himself for noticing anything about her, he said flatly, "You're Prudence Sullivan." It was a statement, not a question, one that only gave her a second to nod in surprise before he continued. "I'm Murdock."

Pru's jaw dropped. *This* was Murdock? This devastatingly handsome, well-put-together hunk was the same jerk who'd yelled at her on the phone yesterday? He couldn't be. There had to be a mistake.

But a second, closer look at those incredible eyes that were lit with expectation, and she knew there was no mistake. This was Murdock, all right, and he was all set to tangle with her like he did every other inspector who crossed his path. More than willing to comply, her gaze shifted to the cement truck fifty yards away before swinging back to him. "Then I guess I don't have to ask who ordered the cement, do I?"

"That's right. I'm in charge around here, and the sooner you get that, the better. Nobody shuts me down, Inspector. Nobody."

It was a taunt, pure and simple, his blue eyes so confident Pru wanted to slug him. Who did he think he was trying to intimidate? She wasn't some piece of fluff who folded like a wimpy house of cards just because a builder dared to challenge her. And the sooner *he* got *that,* the better!

"Waste your money, then," she said airily, a smile starting to flirt with her mouth. "Because if those core tests come back the way I think they will, you're going to have to tear it all out. And if you don't think I can make you do it, then you're not as smart as I heard you are."

They stood nose to nose, the electricity sparking between them so volatile, the air all but sizzled. Her heart slamming against her ribcage, Pru was suddenly struck by the wild, inexplicable need to touch him. Horrified, tantalized, fighting instincts she'd never had for a man in her life, she almost stepped back again. But he could only take that as a weakness and every instinct she possessed told her she was going to have to stand her ground when it came to dealing with this man.

Not budging so much as a muscle, she met his glowering gaze unflinchingly and forced a smile that didn't come as easily as she would have liked. "Do we understand each other, Murdock?"

If she wanted a battle of wills, she had only to look into his grimly determined eyes to know that she had one. Nodding curtly, he said, "Precisely."

Without another word, he stepped around her and walked away, leaving Pru staring after him. Her knees were shaking, her pulse jumping. Later she would be furious that she, who usually treated most men like they were her best buddies, let this one get her hot and bothered without half trying. But for now, all she could think of was that she should have touched him when she'd had the chance.

Two

The music was loud, driving rock, the patrons young and wild. Seated at a table with Laura, Pru stared unseeingly at the energetic dancers crammed onto the dance floor. At any other time she would have found herself a partner and been right out there with the rest of the crowd. But tonight all she could think of was a six foot four hunk of a man who was at least a generation older than the oldest dancer on the floor. He probably wouldn't be caught dead there.

"All right, that's it," Laura said suddenly when Pru sent the sixth good-looking man away like a dog with his tail between his legs. Scandalized by her friend's total disinterest in Grade A prime males, she set her margarita down with a snap and frowned. "You want to tell me what's wrong or do I have to guess?"

Jerked back to her surroundings, Pru blinked in surprise. "What are you talking about? Nothing's wrong."

Laura only snorted at that, unimpressed. "Tell that to someone who doesn't know you so well. Did you even *look* at that guy you just sent packing? He was gorgeous!"

Pru glanced blankly around, unable to even remember what the man looked like. "Was he? I didn't notice."

"I know! That's what I'm talking about. Something's obviously bothering you, Sticks. Come on, what is it? I've never seen you so distracted."

Smiling at the nickname the pint-sized Laura had given her in college, she started to tell her about her crazy fascination with Murdock, only to choke back the words before they escaped. What could she say? *I've met a man who might be old enough to be my father and I think we were meant to be together?* Talk about being a few doughnuts short of a dozen! Laura would think she'd flipped out.

"It's nothing," she hedged, forcing a grimace of a smile. "I was just thinking about work."

Familiar with her problems with Bruce James, Laura immediately jumped to the wrong conclusion. "I knew it! Your boss has been giving you fits again, hasn't he?"

Pru's eyes turned rueful. "I think he lies awake at night dreaming up ways to make me miserable."

Always ready to jump to the defense of a friend, Laura scowled like a ruffled hen. "So what are you going to do about it? There are laws against harassment, you know. Old Brucie baby may not like you, and he probably resents like hell that someone else hired you, but that doesn't mean he can take his frustration out on you. Turn him in."

"He's not an idiot, Shorty. He's made sure he hasn't treated me any differently than anyone else."

Laura nearly strangled on her drink. "You mean he treats *everyone* like dirt?"

"Just about."

Pru started to tell her about how Eric Thompson was fired, but she'd hardly begun when a tall, blond man appeared at her side and grinned down at her as if she'd been put on this earth just for him. "Hi, sugar. How 'bout a dance?"

Pru almost rolled her eyes and sent him packing with the rest. But Laura gave her a pointed look and, with a resigned shrug, she rose to her feet. "Sure. Why not?"

For the next three hours she danced just about every dance and really did have a good time. Refusing to take any of her partners too seriously, she laughed at their jokes, shrugged off their flattery and graciously turned down all dates. And when she finally went home, she went alone, just as she always did.

It wasn't that she wasn't interested in dating or finding a man of her own, she admitted as she let herself into her silent apartment and got ready for bed. She would love to have a husband and a real, honest-to-God home of her own with the man she adored. And children.

Something shifted deep inside her, something soft and tender and sweet, at the thought of a child. *Her* child. She could almost see it, a beautiful baby, its tiny features a fascinating combination of hers and its daddy's, a treasured symbol of their love for each other. And if she closed her eyes and totally emptied her mind, she was sure it was only a matter of time before she caught a glimpse of *him,* the man who was going to give her that child.

But when she climbed into bed and closed her eyes, the only man she saw was Zebadiah Murdock.

She groaned, the defeated sound loud in the dark, quiet stillness of her lonely bedroom. She would *not* do this! she promised herself. The infuriating man had dominated her thoughts enough for one evening. It had to stop!

Flopping over onto her stomach, she punched her pillow into just the right shape and closed her eyes with a tired sigh. Exhaustion from a long, tense day of work and then hours of dancing came out of nowhere to swamp her senses. Her breathing slow and regular, she never knew when sleep overtook her.

Or when Murdock walked into her dreams.

Her defenses down, she never thought to question his presence there. He was just there, where he'd always belonged. Her lover throughout eternity, her soul mate, the man she was meant to go through time with, as much a part of her being as the familiar beating of her heart.

Entranced, she watched in fascination as a white mist swirled around him, obliterating him from view before suddenly parting to reveal the two of them together. Her breath caught in her throat, longing swelling in her as she watched herself move into his arms and gracefully dance to the faint strains of a melody that was hauntingly familiar.

Murmuring his name, she reached for the sensuous image, needing, just for one heart-stopping moment, to hold on to it. But her fingers encountered nothing but the empty space beside her in the bed and she came awake abruptly, the sensuous dream swept away on a devastating tidal wave of loss.

You've been waiting for him more lifetimes than you can remember, an unknown voice echoed in her head. *Don't let him get away.*

Her heart thundering as if she'd just run a mile, Pru rolled onto her back and found herself blinking back hot, ridiculous tears. Stunned, she lifted her fingers to her cheeks and stared at the moisture that clung to them. Tears, she thought dazedly. She was crying for Murdock!

And hearing voices. Dear God, what was happening to her? she thought in growing hysteria. Murdock didn't even like her! And she wasn't actually crazy about him, either. So how could she dream about him, ache for him, picture a future with him?

You've been waiting for him for more lifetimes than you can remember.

The softly spoken words whispered through her consciousness, sounding so familiar she would have sworn she'd heard them before. But where? When? Agitated, her stomach churning, she got out of bed. Without bothering to turn on a light, she started to pace restlessly in the dark. It was just a bad case of lust at first sight, she reasoned. An experienced woman would have recognized that immediately, but then again, she was hardly what anyone with even a smidgen of brains would call experienced. Up until now the men in her life had just been friends, pals, big brothers. Not a one of them had so much as raised her temper, let alone her temperature. So how could she have possibly known that physical attraction could be as volatile as a charge of lightning in an unstable sky? No wonder she couldn't handle it.

But lust didn't explain the mysterious voice in her head. Sweet, loving, sure, it spoke with a conviction she couldn't shake. And that, more than anything, was what scared her. She wasn't one of those imaginative, daydreaming women with her head in the clouds all the time. She was practical right down to her white cotton underwear, and she didn't believe in fairy tales, reincarnation, or voices that spoke to her in the middle of the night. So why was her heart knocking like crazy in her breast?

Feeling as if she was losing it, she threw herself across the bed, reached for the phone on the nightstand and quickly dialed Kansas City. It wasn't until she heard her mother's sleepy voice on the other end of the line that she glanced at the bedside clock. "Oh, God, Mom, I'm sorry! I didn't realize the time—"

"Prudence?" Cynthia Sullivan gasped in alarm. "It's after two! What's wrong? Are you all right? You never call this late."

Already hearing the panic in her mother's voice, Pru wanted to kick herself for not checking the time before picking up the phone. "It's nothing," she assured her quickly. "I'll call you back in the morning."

Her mother only clicked her tongue at that nonsense and said dryly, "This is your mother you're talking to, honey. I know when something's wrong—I can hear it in your voice. Why don't you tell me what it is?"

In the background, Pru could hear the grandfather clock down the hall from her parents' bedroom striking the hour. Suddenly homesick, she could do nothing to stop the sudden tears that stung her eyes. "This is so screwy." She laughed shakily, swallowing the lump in her throat. "I don't even know where to start."

Like a dam that had suddenly cracked open, the words came pouring out in a jumbled rush, unedited and flustered. "I don't know what's wrong with me," she said after describing the dream and her working relationship with Murdock. "I hardly know the man, and he definitely doesn't like me. And then that voice...I tell you, Mom, I think I'm losing it."

Cynthia Sullivan laughed gaily. "Honey, you're not losing anything! Didn't I ever tell you about the first time I saw your father? I knew right then he was the man for me."

"But what about the voice? And all this stuff about different lifetimes?"

"Who knows? It's a strange world, sweetheart, and some things just can't be explained. The question is, how do you feel about Murdock?"

Pru hesitated, but the truth wouldn't be denied. "I don't know," she blurted. "I just know my heart started skipping the minute I laid eyes on him and I can't get him out of my head. And now he's in my dreams."

"Then maybe you should find a way to get better acquainted with him," her mother suggested. "If you're still fascinated with him after you get to know him, you may have just found the man of your dreams."

She made it sound so easy. "Was it that simple for you and Daddy?"

Even through the phone line, she could hear the smile in her mother's voice. "It was just like falling off a log, honey. We couldn't help ourselves. And if you and Murdock are made for each other, it will be that easy for you, too."

Pru wanted to believe her, but long after she hung up and went back to bed, she lay in the dark, too restless to go back to sleep, her thoughts tangled and unsure. Images flashed before her mind's eye, images that were part of her dream, part of what could be. Her and Murdock together...always. The whole idea was crazy. *She* was crazy. But for some reason she couldn't explain, it felt right. She didn't know where a possible friendship with him would lead, but she had to find out. She wanted to get to know the man, to figure out what made him tick . . . and turned him on.

Feeling like she'd already waited forever, Pru wanted to put her plan into action immediately, but it wasn't that easy. When she arrived at the site the next morning, Murdock was already there, defiantly pouring cement, his smile mocking as he silently dared her to just try to stop him. She didn't. Instead she walked right up to him and offered him her hand. "We got off on the wrong foot yesterday," she said easily, and had the satisfaction of seeing his eyes narrow suspiciously. Suddenly wanting to laugh, she struggled to hold back a grin. "So I thought we could shake hands and start over."

His eyes locked on her hand, Murdock didn't move, didn't so much as blink. He didn't want to touch her, didn't even want to think about touching her. But they were in full view of his crew and there was no way he could avoid accepting her handshake without looking like a jerk. Reluctantly, his fingers closed around hers.

The heat was instantaneous, like the flare of a match, jumping from his hand to hers. Startled, he felt it and knew she did, too. He watched her eyes fly to their joined hands, felt her fingers tremble and his own heart slam against his ribs. With a muttered curse, he jerked his hand back, but it didn't do much good. He still burned.

Pru blinked and looked down at her hand as if she'd never seen it before. "Well," she said, her voice catching revealingly, "I guess that takes care of the formalities. Maybe now we can be friends."

But when she looked back at Murdock, he only nodded stiffly, his shuttered expression not giving her much encouragement. "Sure. Now, if you'll excuse me, I've got to get back to work."

It wasn't the response she'd hoped for, but it was a start and not all that bad a one, she decided, considering how he felt about inspectors. Just because she generally knew what she wanted the minute she saw it didn't mean that he did. She just had to give him some time. After all, it wasn't as if either one of them was going anywhere. The project was a long way from being finished, and they would be dealing with each other every day. It would be much easier for both of them if they could manage to become friends.

But even though he'd agreed to start over, it soon became apparent that he really had no intention of doing anything of the kind. He was an attractive man and when he was dealing with anyone but her, he actually smiled and laughed. For the first time in her life, envy stirred in her, turning her eyes greener than normal, and she didn't like it. She knew she was being ridiculous— she hardly knew him. But she wanted him to be as relaxed with her as he was with his crew. She wanted him to see *her* when he looked at her—Pru Sullivan, the woman, not an inspector he was forced to tolerate. And she wanted him to smile at her, just once, as if he meant it.

But it didn't happen. The results of the core samples came in and the numbers were acceptable, but only by a hairbreadth. Murdock, so sure the test results would come back heavily in his favor, was shocked and grudgingly admitted that the test was justified. He could no longer deny that she knew what she was doing, but that didn't mean he had to be happy about it. Because every time she found something wrong, he just had another problem to solve.

For the next three days he continued to look through her instead of at her. Then, just when she thought she was going to have to grab the man by the ears and shake him to get his attention, she discovered that the electricians he had hired to wire the entire complex were not using American-made materials.

It was a mistake that shouldn't have been made. Regulations required that the majority of materials used on government projects had to be American-made. She might have been able to believe another contractor doing a government job for the first time might not have known that. But not Murdock. He was too sharp to make that kind of costly mistake.

There had to be another explanation, she decided. She'd heard about the problems on the site, problems that evidently went all the way back to the first day when ground was broken. Other, less reputable builders had those kinds of problems all the time. Zebadiah Murdock, however, had a reputation that was head and shoulders above such men. From what she'd heard around the site, he didn't normally have those kinds of headaches. So what was wrong? It was time she found out.

Not looking forward to the coming conversation, she went looking for Murdock and found him standing outside his minuscule office with his back to her, talking to Roy Wilkins. Her heart lurching in its now familiar way at the sight of him, Pru had eyes for no one but Murdock. She hadn't been this close to him all day, and for a moment she completely forgot why she had sought him out.

Then Roy saw her and stopped talking in midsentence.

Surprised, Murdock whirled to see who'd approached and just barely bit back a groan. He'd been trying to ignore her for days now, but even if she hadn't been the only woman at the site, she was hard to miss. She always seemed to be just within the corner of his vision, impossible to overlook. And even harder to forget. Every night when he went home, she was right there with him in his head.

And for the life of him, he didn't know why. Just because he was a confirmed bachelor at forty-five didn't mean he was a recluse. When he was in need of female companionship, there were any number of women he could call. Women who were older, more mature, women whose interests matched his. Women, when he thought of Pru, he didn't call. It was irritating as hell.

Ignoring the sudden heat in the air that hadn't been there seconds before, he never took his eyes from Pru as he told his field superintendent, "We'll talk about this later, Roy. Go ahead and take a break. I'll find you after I'm through with Inspector Sullivan."

Roy, witness to more than one of their *discussions,* was quick to cut and run. In the tense silence left by his leave-taking, Murdock drawled, "Don't tell me. You've gone over everything with a magnifying glass and you've finally found something to complain about. What is it this time? Measurements a thousandth of a millimeter off, or what?"

The quick retort that sprang to her tongue caught between her teeth, Pru only grinned. The last time she'd let a male push her buttons, she'd been twelve and Tommy Stinson had teased her for being flat-chested while all her friends were blooming like roses. She'd socked him then and learned the value of taking a man by surprise.

"Actually, I was wondering if you'd like to go to lunch with me," she said easily, flashing her dimples at him. "What do you say? Are you game?"

Murdock couldn't have been more stunned if she'd tossed a bucket of wet cement over his head. His brows snapping together, he eyed her warily. "For what?"

"Either it's been a long time since a woman has asked you to lunch or I'm not doing it right. Lunch," she laughed. "I'm talking about lunch. You know... food...that meal you eat in the middle of the day?"

"Let's just put it this way," he retorted. "It's been a long time since an *inspector's* invited me to lunch. This is business, isn't it?"

The truth hovering on her tongue, Pru almost told him no. The only business she wanted to discuss with him was a fascination that wouldn't go away. But he obviously wasn't prepared to hear that, so she had no choice but to agree. "Of course," she said as if she'd never thought of suggesting anything else. "We need to talk about some of the problems you've been having here on the site and I thought the discussion would be less tense on neutral ground."

It was a plausible excuse and one that Pru thought sounded darn good. But she saw in a glance that Murdock wasn't buying it. He just looked at her and said dryly, "Thanks, but no thanks. You know how guys talk. We go off together and it's going to be all over the site that I'm kissing up to the inspector. If you want to talk, we can do it right here in my office."

Pru wanted to object—spending time with him on the job was *not* what she wanted!—but he didn't give her the chance. Turning, he jerked open the door to his cracker box of an office and patiently waited for her to precede him. Ruefully accepting defeat, she gave in gracefully and stepped into the small, portable building.

Pru had been in her share of site offices and knew from firsthand experience that they were usually crowded and messy, with hardly enough room to turn around. Murdock's was no different except for the fact that paperwork littering the desk that took up most of the available floor space was neatly stacked and organized.

Impressed, she lifted a brow in surprise, amusement glinting in her eyes as she turned to tease him about his neatness fetish. But the door shut behind him as he followed her inside, and in the blink of an eye he was right in front of her, so close she could practically feel the sharp breath he drew in in surprise. Between one heartbeat and the next, the playful words hovering on her tongue turned to dust.

Trapped between the desk at her back and Murdock's hard, lean body in front of her, Pru felt her heart start to knock against her ribs. Still, she couldn't move, didn't want to. Lord, how could she have known just standing this close to him could turn her knees to water? Light-headed, her blood racing through her veins with an anticipation she couldn't explain, she found herself holding her breath, waiting, waiting for his arms to slip around her. Somehow she knew it was going to be the best thing that ever happened to her.

But he didn't touch her.

He didn't dare.

The air suddenly thick with sexual tension, Murdock stared down at her, his hands curled into fists at his sides. He never should have let her anywhere near his office, he thought too late. It was too small, too private, and she was much, much too close. If he leaned the slightest bit toward her...

He'd be in big trouble. Because something warned him that once he gave in to the need to touch her, she'd be nearly impossible to walk away from.

Fighting the outrageous need to reach for her, he abruptly stepped around her to get to his desk, his jaw hardening when his arm accidentally brushed against her. Just as when he'd been forced to shake hands with her, heat stirred, stealing the moisture from his mouth, stunning him. And her. Again. Her face an open book, she met his gaze wide-eyed, hiding nothing of her thoughts. And what he saw in her eyes shook him to the core. Dammit, didn't she know better than to look at a man the way she was looking at him? As if he was the next best thing to sliced bread and she couldn't get over the wonder of him? God Almighty, couldn't she see he was too old for her?

He reached the comparative safety behind his desk, but it didn't help. There just wasn't enough room in the small office to put any real space between them. And how the hell was he supposed to keep his mind on business when that perfume of hers was guaranteed to drive him slowly out of his mind?

With a jerk of his hand, he motioned to the sturdy metal chair angled across from his desk. "Sit down," he growled, then settled into the old leather office chair that he'd used at every building site for the last twenty years. "All right, you wanted to talk, so talk. What's the problem?"

Any hope that Pru had had that they might, for once, have a nice, friendly conversation died a swift death at his cool tone. His eyes were dark with distrust, his mouth set and unsmiling. He even glanced pointedly at the clock, silently reminding her that she was wasting precious time. It shouldn't have hurt—she'd known getting past the hostility he kept between them like a shield wouldn't be easy—but it did.

Sternly ordering herself not to be so sensitive, she met his gaze unflinchingly. "I think it's time you told me what's going on around here, don't you?"

In the process of reaching for a pencil, Murdock froze. "Going on? What are you talking about?"

"I would think that was obvious," she retorted. "I'm not deaf, you know. I've heard the stories about the project and all the problems you've had. The tool thefts, the vandalism, the unacceptable materials—"

He stopped her right there. "Pick any building site in this city and you're going to run into some type of theft and vandalism. It just goes with the territory, especially in today's world. As for problems with materials, I don't know what you're talking about. True, there was a mix-up with the cement, but it was within the acceptable limits."

Pulling a piece of the foreign-made wiring she'd found earlier out of her pocket, she tossed it onto his desk. "This has nothing to do with cement. You'd better look at this."

A licensed electrician, Murdock knew before his fingers ever closed over the small length of wiring that it wasn't anything he'd ordered for the Fort Sam project. "Where did you get this?" he demanded sharply, glancing up. "I didn't buy this."

"Then why are your electricians using it all over the site?"

"They're not," he snapped. "Roy ordered all American-made materials for this job, including the electrical supplies, then inspected them himself when they came in. If there'd been a problem, he would have told me immediately and corrected it."

"Then someone's pulled a fast one on the two of you," she replied. "Because right now the east wing's wired with this and I can't pass it until it's changed."

"The hell it is!"

"I'm sorry, Murdock, but it is. If you don't believe me, go look for yourself."

He was already on his feet, stepping around his desk. "All right, I will. Let's go."

Following her outside, his long legs quickly carried him to the east wing where the electricians had started roughing in the wiring the second the cement had been approved. Another shorter woman would have had a difficult time keeping up with him, but Pru's legs were only a few inches shorter than his and she matched him stride for stride. So when he stepped inside the shell of a building and inspected the wiring that was already in place and soon to be concealed behind Sheetrock, she was right there with him.

"Son of a bitch!"

The softly snarled curse echoed like a scream in the empty building. Watching him closely, Pru slowly released the breath she had been unobtrusively holding, any doubts that Murdock might have known of the subterfuge vanishing when she saw the fury in his eyes.

"Have you checked the rest of this wing?"

She jumped when he turned on her suddenly, his blue eyes dark and piercing. She saw in an instant that he wasn't mad at her, but at whoever did this. And she didn't want to be in their shoes when he caught up with them. The fur was going to fly.

She nodded. "It's all the same."

He cursed again, a low, fluent damnation of the bonehead who didn't know the difference between American and imported wiring. "What about the material that hasn't been installed, yet?" he asked tersely. "Have you checked that?"

"No, of course not. I only inspect the work in progress and after it's finished."

"Then let's go check it out."

With her at his side, he hurried outside and crossed to the stockpile of supplies that were stacked high under sheets of protective plastic. Tossing the plastic out of the way, he found the wiring right where it was supposed to be. A single glance told him all he needed to know. It wasn't made in the U.S.A.

Three

———

Stunned, feeling like someone had sucker punched him in a kidney, Murdock never knew how long he stood there staring in disbelief at the useless wiring. His teeth locked on a string of unprintable curses, he didn't make a sound, but the rage building in him must have been apparent because Pru suddenly reached over and touched the tensed muscles of his forearm.

"It could just be an innocent mix-up," she said hopefully. "Someone else's order probably got delivered here by mistake. It happens all the time. You can straighten it out with a few phone calls."

The lines bracketing his mouth deepening, Murdock knew the mistake couldn't be explained—or corrected—that simply. Sure, screwups happened. But this project had had more than its fair share and each one hit him right where it hurt the most—in the pocket-book. If it didn't stop, and damn soon, he'd be lucky to walk away from the job with the shirt on his back.

"I'll take care of it," he told her grimly. "And don't worry about the east wing. It'll be rewired, of course." Letting out a heavy sigh, his eyes met hers. "It looks like I owe you an apology. Oh, yes, I do," he insisted when she started to shake her head. "I did everything but accuse you of lying."

"You've been under a lot of stress," she said quickly, disturbed at the thought of him apologizing to her for something that was perfectly understandable considering their adversarial working relationship. "With everything that's been going on around here, who can blame you?"

His lips starting to twitch, Murdock gazed down at her. "Let me get this straight. *You're* making excuses for me being a jackass?"

Put that way, Pru couldn't help but laugh. "Yeah, I guess I am."

Her sexy laughter rolling over him like a heat wave, Murdock knew it was a sound that would haunt his dreams if he didn't put some distance between them, and damn soon. Before the thought had fully formed, he took a step away from her. "Well, you don't have to, but I appreciate your understanding." His voice too husky, he took another quick step. "I've got to find Roy and see how this happened without anyone noticing. Thanks for your help."

Leaving her with her own reports to file, he went in search of Roy and found him deep in a conversation with one of the plumbing subcontractors. He'd been Murdock's right-hand man for more than five years. In all that time he'd never missed a day of work. He'd also never screwed up on a supply order. Murdock couldn't believe he had this time, either. He was too dependable, too good at what he did. So what the hell had happened?

He was still asking himself that same question a few minutes later when the plumber went back to work. Roy turned toward him, took one look at his stony expression, and groaned. "Don't tell me. We flunked another inspection."

Murdock nodded. "The wiring in the east wing. It's not American-made."

"What? You've got to be kidding! It has to be. I ordered it myself."

His words rang true enough, but it wasn't what he said that concerned Murdock. It was his eyes. In his years in the construction business, he'd met his share of crooks and swindlers, and he'd become pretty damn good at spotting a lie in a man's eyes. If Roy's confused puzzlement was an act, he was in the wrong business. With that kind of talent, he should have been in Hollywood.

Just that quickly, a suspicion he hadn't allowed himself to acknowledge shriveled up and died, abruptly easing the tension that knotted the muscles at the back of his neck. Relieved, he expelled a short breath and asked, "What exactly did you order?"

"Just what you put in the specs."

"That's not what was delivered."

"The hell it wasn't! You know I always double-check the supplies when they come in, and everything checked out. I've got the receipts to prove it."

"Then we've got a bigger problem than I thought," he said grimly. Quickly and succinctly, he told him about what he and Pru had discovered when they'd inspected the cache of supplies. "If the correct supplies were delivered like you say, then that can only mean one thing. Someone stole the right wiring and replaced it with the imported so the theft wouldn't be noticed. Someone who knew the foreign stuff would be worthless to us."

Jerking off his hard hat to wipe his sweating brow, Roy shot him a hard look. "You think it's one of the workers?"

"I don't know."

Glancing at the crew that worked around them, he didn't want to think that someone on his payroll was responsible for the theft. He'd worked with most of the men on and off for years. He knew their families, had been to their homes, had even, on occasion, loaned a few of them money when they'd gotten themselves in a tight financial spot. He couldn't believe any of them would steal from him, lie to him.

But a common thief wouldn't know the difference between American- and foreign-made materials. And if he was a junkie looking for something to hock to get his next fix, he sure as hell wouldn't go to the time and expense of replacing what he'd stolen. No, the problems he'd had from the first day ground had been broken couldn't be blamed on a sticky-fingered stranger. Only someone who knew construction could cause this much trouble. And only someone who had it in for him would. Now all he had to figure out was which one of the dozens of the crewmen he considered friends was working against him. And why.

"At this point, we can't rule out anyone," he said tersely. "Whoever it is, they'd damn well better enjoy themselves while they can, because their days are numbered. I'll nail them even if I have to go the expense of putting in surveillance cameras to do it."

Hoping it didn't come to that, he made a few phone calls and, within an hour, he had a fencing company at the site to fence the entire area. The M.P.'s were notified of the theft and promised to increase hourly patrols. It was some consolation, but Murdock was through taking chances. By the end of the workday, he watched in satisfaction as two Dobermans were delivered by their trainer and locked in the fenced area, just as they would be every night until the project was finished.

It was Friday night and he'd done all he could do. The increased security drew comments from some of the crew, but he only shrugged and explained that he was worried about vandalism because of some increased criminal activity in the area. The thief, whoever he was, had to know better; he didn't reveal his identity by so much as a flicker of an eyelash.

"Hey, Murdock, you comin' or not?"

In the process of locking up his office, Murdock glanced over his shoulder to find Bill Dancer waiting expectantly. If it had been anyone else but Bill, he would have told him to stuff it, he wasn't going anywhere. But he and Bill went back a long way, to the days when they'd both been young and wild and reckless, and he was the oldest friend he had.

"Where, you old reprobate? You come dragging in late on payday and Tracy's going to have your hide."

Unconcerned, Bill just grinned, the laugh lines at the corner of his eyes crinkling. "Nah—the woman's crazy about me. So, are you going to Charlie's or not? There's a game tonight."

Murdock grimaced. He'd forgotten.

A popular sports bar on the north side of town, Charlie's was the usual meeting place of most of the crew whenever the San Antonio Spurs were playing a basketball game that was broadcast on pay-per-view on cable. For the cost of a couple of beers, they could watch the game on a big-screen TV and eat all the free hors d'oeuvres they could hold. For a bunch of construction workers who could eat just about anyone under the table, that was too good a deal to pass up.

As big a fan as the rest of the crew, he normally enjoyed the games and those nights out with his men. But for the past two hours, all he'd thought about was getting home and stretching out on his couch in front of his own TV with a cold beer. Not really in the mood for company, he almost made an excuse and let Bill and the rest of the guys go without him. But the men weren't stupid. They knew about the problems on site and had noted the added security. If he started avoiding them, they'd begin to wonder which one of them he didn't trust. Morale wouldn't be worth spit.

So it looked like he was going to Charlie's. "Yeah, I guess I can make it. You're not going to get us thrown out of the place again, are you?"

"Who, me?" His brown eyes twinkling innocently, Bill's smile was devilishly wicked. "I'm an old married man. I wouldn't do something like that."

Murdock snorted, his lips twitching with amusement. "Yeah, right. Tell that to someone who doesn't know you so well."

"I can't. Nobody knows me as well as you do." Chuckling, he slapped him on the shoulder. "Tip-off's at seven-thirty. See you there, buddy. I've got to catch Pru before she leaves."

Surprised, Murdock swore, but it was too late. Bill was already hurrying to catch up with Pru.

"Hey, Pru," he called out. "You got plans for to-night?"

Standing at her Jeep and digging in her purse for her keys, Pru looked up to see Bill sprinting toward her. Hoping Murdock's hostility toward her wouldn't spill over to his men, she'd spent the past few days making friends with the crew. She'd thought she'd been care-ful—she knew the dangers of working with a bunch of men and how easily it was for some of them to take her friendliness for a come-on when it was nothing of the kind. But now, as Bill's words registered, it was obvi-ous she'd gone too far. And he wasn't the man she'd thought he was—he'd made no secret of the fact that he was married.

Disappointed that she'd misread him, she began, "Well, as a matter of fact, I—"

"Aw, come on, don't say no," he cut in quickly, an-ticipating her refusal. "Most of the guys are meeting at Charlie's Sports Bar a little later to watch the Spurs game on TV, and I thought you might like to come along, too."

"Oh!" Cringing at her overactive imagination, she prayed he didn't see the heat climbing in her cheeks. "That's not too far from where I live. Who all's go-ing?"

Appalled, Pru listened in horror as the words blithely tripped off her tongue, but it was too late to take them back. Dear God, what was she doing? From the first day she'd reported to work, Bruce James had warned her that he would consider any fraternizing with the men whose work she would be inspecting a serious conflict of interest. If she so much as dared to flirt with one, she'd be out on her ear. And now she was actually thinking about going out with the whole group? Skinny-necked James was going to have a stroke!

"And Miguel, Sam, Jason," Bill rattled on blithely, unaware she was already regretting giving him the least encouragement. "Oh, yeah, and Murdock's going," he added. "I just talked to him and he's going to meet all of us out there around seven-thirty."

Expectation rippled through Pru, sweet and exhilarating and tempting as sin. Automatically she glanced past Bill's shoulder to the site office, only to have her gaze slam into Murdock's. Startled, her breath caught in her throat, surprise weakening her knees. He was watching her. Standing as still as a mountain in the late afternoon shadows cast by the small portable building that served as his office, he gazed at her unblinkingly.

Fascinated, unable to look away from him, she watched a frown inch its ways across his brow and knew what he was thinking as clearly as if one of the powers that be suddenly linked her mind with his. From fifty yards away he couldn't possibly hear what Bill was saying to her, but somehow he knew she was being included in the night out with the boys. And even though she'd managed to drag a smile out of him earlier, he was none-too-thrilled about spending an evening with her. His hard gaze warned her not to even think about accepting Bill's invitation.

He was all but daring her to show up, she realized, her eyes starting to twinkle. The poor baby had no idea she'd always had a teensy-weensy problem with dares. She just couldn't resist them. Or the chance to go out with him, even if there would be ten other guys along.

Turning back to Bill, she gave him a brilliant smile. "You know, that does sound like fun. What time does the game start?"

"Seven-thirty."

"Great! I'll see you and the rest of the guys then."
Ignoring Murdock's fierce scowl of disapproval, she
struggled to hold back laughter as she boldly gave him
a teasing wave and climbed into her Jeep. As she drove
away and glanced into her rearview mirror, she almost
choked on a giggle. He hadn't moved. And he was still
frowning.

She had less than two hours to change into something more suitable than khaki work clothes, then get
over to Charlie's. She wasted forty-five minutes of that
trying on practically everything in her closet. But nothing looked or felt right. Disgusted, she finally called
Laura. "Help! I'm going out and I haven't got the fog-
giest idea what to wear."

"Well, it's about time." Laura laughed. "I'll be right
there."

She was as good as her word, and ten minutes later
she was walking into Pru's bedroom. She took one look
at the clothes tossed haphazardly around Pru's usually
neat room and lifted a delicately arched brow in surprise. "Okay, give. Who is he?"

"Who?"

"The guy you're going out with. The one who's got
you all in a tizzy. You didn't throw clothes around when
you went out with John Styles when we were in college,
and he was the best-looking hunk on campus. So name
names, Sticks. Tell me everything."

Grinning, Pru held up her fingers and started to
count them off. "Bill, Miguel, Sam, Jason—"

"Okay, okay, you made your point," Laura cut in
with pretended huffiness. "You don't want to tell me.
Fine. I can handle it."

Pru laughed, not fooled in the least. Laura was like a hound after a fox when she was on the trail of some good gossip, and she wouldn't quit until she got the answers she wanted. "I'm just meeting some of the guys from work at a sports bar to watch the Spurs game. It's no big deal. And if I don't find something to wear, I'm not even going to go."

Laura knew her too well to swallow that fish story whole. Her cheerleader-cute face alive with mischief, she teased, "He must be something special if he's got you so stirred up you don't even know what to wear. What's his name? Come on, tell Auntie Laura all about him. You know you're dying to."

Unable to hold back a laugh, Pru frowned at her in affectionate exasperation. "Did anyone ever tell you you're like a dog with a bone? His name's Murdock—"

Her eyes wide as saucers, Laura almost swallowed her tongue. "*The* Murdock of Murdock Construction?"

Pru nodded. "The one and only. And he wants nothing to do with me. So don't start planning the wedding just yet, okay."

"What do you mean, he wants nothing to do with you?" she demanded, bristling indignantly. "Is he blind, or what?"

"No, I think he's my soul mate," she retorted, and for the first time in recent memory, she had the satisfaction of seeing Laura stunned speechless. "Now that you know why I'm so shook up, could you help me find something to wear? There's a lot riding on tonight."

Recovering quickly, Laura wasn't about to let her drop that bombshell, then change the subject. Her smile fading, she said quietly, "You're serious, aren't you?"

"Yeah," she admitted huskily. "I know it sounds crazy. I took one look at the man and I just...knew. It was like getting run over by a truck."

"But *soul mates,* Sticks? That's heavy stuff. And you've never even been out with him, have you? How can you possibly know?"

Pru asked herself the same question night after night when she dreamed about him, but the answer was still as elusive as he was. "I don't know. I just do. I can't explain how or why, but I feel like I've been waiting for him all my life."

If anyone else had said such a thing to her, Laura would have dismissed them as a diehard romantic who fell in and out of love as easily as most people got in and out of bed. But she knew Prudence Sullivan as well as she knew herself, and she wasn't the kind of woman who indulged in flights of fantasy. Her feet were firmly planted on the ground, and as far as Laura knew, she'd never once been tempted to give her heart to any man. Until now.

Shaking off her bemusement, she said, "Well, then, we'd better find you something super to wear so you can knock this guy out of his shoes."

With half her clothes already tossed on the bed and floor, Pru was sure she didn't have anything appropriate. Watching Laura quickly shift through the items that remained in her closet, she was half tempted to call the whole thing off. What had ever possessed her to agree to this, anyway? Bars weren't her scene. For that matter, neither was dating. Oh, she'd gone out before, of course, for a pizza or movie or even a concert, but that was with friends who just happened to be men. She hadn't been nervous, and she certainly hadn't lost any sleep over them after they'd brought her home. But then again, none of them had been Murdock.

Panic seizing her by the throat, she almost chickened out then and there. She could stay home with a good book and completely avoid the anxiety already twisting in her gut just at the thought of walking into Charlie's and making small talk with Murdock. But then she pictured herself facing Bill and the crew on Monday, trying to explain why she'd been a no-show, and she couldn't come up with a single plausible excuse.

She had to go. Deep in her heart, something stronger than herself warned her she would regret it the rest of her life if she let this opportunity—and Murdock—slip away from her just because she was a coward. All right, so most people had learned to deal with this kind of anxiety when they were sixteen, she ruefully acknowledged. So what? She was a late bloomer. The tallest one in her class from first grade until her junior year, she'd been self-conscious of her height around boys. And that wasn't something you got over overnight. Which was why, at age twenty-eight, she wanted to get a man's attention for the first time in her life and didn't have a clue as to how to go about doing it. Lord, what was she going to do?

Too nervous to just stand there and wait for Laura to find her something to wear, she started picking up the clothes she'd carelessly dropped on the bed. "I feel like a teenager going out on a blind date for the first time," she grumbled as she hung a blouse back on its hanger. "I know I'm going to make a fool of myself. I don't even know what to say to him."

"You'll do fine," Laura assured her as she stepped out of her closet with a white blouse and her best pair of black jeans. "If nothing else, talk about the game.

And you can always get him to talk about himself. Just cater to his ego. It'll be a piece of cake. Here, try these on and let's see how you look."

A few minutes later, doubts churning in her stomach and her heart thumping madly, Pru stood in front of the full-length mirror attached to the bathroom door and shook her head. "I don't know. Don't you think I need something a little flashier? He's not even going to look twice at me in this getup, especially when there's a game on TV."

"Are you kidding?" Laura laughed. "You look like a million bucks! The poor man's not going to be able to keep his eyes off you. And neither is any other man in the joint. So quit worrying. You've got it made in the shade."

Pru wanted to believe her, but when she approached the front door of the sports bar an hour later, she almost turned around and left without going inside. She'd spotted Murdock's pickup in the parking lot, along with most of the rest of the crew's, and her knees started to knock just at the thought of walking inside and joining him. But before she could actually cut and run, another patron approached and held the door for her and she had no choice but to step inside.

Feeling as if she'd just made a decision that was going to irrevocably change her life, she moved out of the flow of incoming traffic and stopped right inside the front door to scout her surroundings. The place was big and noisy, with pool tables taking up an elevated area on the right, a long bar on the left, and in the middle, a large-screen TV that was currently exposing the pre-game show. And right in front of the TV were three tables that had been pushed together by the Fort Sam construction crew.

The whole crowd was there—Bill and Roy and the rest of the men, some with dates—all of them laughing and talking and snacking on the free munchies as they waited for the game to start. But the only one she had eyes for was Murdock.

As always, her heart lurched at the sight of him. He was half turned away from her, the beer he held lifted halfway to his mouth as he grinned at something Roy had just said. He hadn't seen her, so for once, she gave in to temptation and looked her fill. Lord, he was something to see!

Like the rest of the crew, he'd obviously gone home straight from work to shower and change, and if Pru hadn't known better, she would have sworn she could smell the fresh, spicy scent of his after-shave from where she stood halfway across the bar. Dressed in blue Dockers and a blue-and-white striped polo shirt, his black hair just brushing his brow and the top of his collar, he was the best-looking man in the place.

Given the opportunity, Pru could have watched him for hours. But almost as if he sensed her watching him, his smile faltered and he suddenly turned toward the entrance. Before she could glance away, his gaze locked with hers and he found her staring at him.

She should have moved then, looked away, done anything but stand there and look at him while the world around her faded from her awareness. For all she knew, time itself could have ceased to exist. Somewhere on the edge of her consciousness she knew she was starting to draw amused glances, but they didn't register. Nothing did but the thundering echo in her ears that was her own heartbeat and the man who sat forty feet away from her and gazed into her soul. Unable to stay away, she started toward him.

He watched her every step of the way. He'd spent the past two hours convincing himself that he could easily spend the evening with her without even breaking a sweat. After all, it wasn't as if he would have to be alone with her. His men would be there, and most of the time would be spent watching the game. It would be a piece of cake.

But the Pru slowly bearing down on him was not the same woman who had driven away from the Fort Sam site just a few hours ago. That Pru had been every inch the inspector, right down to her khakis and work boots. This Pru was something else, a woman he'd never seen before. She'd ditched the dull clothes like a butterfly shedding its cocoon and with very little effort had achieved an artless femininity that she didn't even seem to be aware of.

And for the life of him, Murdock didn't know how she did it. Her clothes weren't all that provocative or fancy; she just wore black jeans and a white shirt. But the jeans hugged her incredibly long legs, the metallic silver belt that she wore with them drawing the eye to an impossibly small waist. And the blouse was . . . dangerous, he decided in a single, all-encompassing glance, taking in the way it draped her breasts. Made from some kind of soft, crushable material, it had a rounded, ruffled neckline that bared her vulnerable neck before meeting in the center, where it tied. Just wondering what it would feel like to untie her like a present was enough to heat his blood.

Suddenly realizing that he was all but stripping her with his eyes, he snapped his teeth together on an oath and quickly looked away. But it didn't help. He seemed to have radar where she was concerned and knew the exact moment she reached the table. Every nerve in his body seemed to tighten in response.

"Hi, guys," she said in a voice that made him think of silk sheets and dark, moonless nights. "Looks like I'm the last one here. You got room for one more?"

"Sure," Roy said easily as the others all greeted her. Always the gentleman, he was already on his feet. "Here, Pru. Take my seat. I'll get another one. Move over, guys. The game's starting."

Everyone stood up, another chair was dragged over and squeezed in with the rest, and somehow in the shuffle Murdock found himself seated next to Pru. On the television, the announcer started the play-by-play as the opening jump ball was tossed into the air, but under the table, Pru's leg accidentally brushed his and he stared blankly at the large screen without seeing a thing.

Tension tightening every muscle in his body, he tried his damnedest to ignore her, but she made that impossible. Leaning forward during one particularly exciting slam dunk, she laughed and clapped with the rest of the crew and never seemed to notice how her left shoulder was crowding his. But he noticed. Lord, did he ever! The soft, bare skin of her upper arm barely grazed his shirt sleeve, yet he felt the sparks shoot all the way to the tips of his fingers and he almost dropped his mug of beer.

And then there was her perfume. God, had he ever smelled anything like it in his life? It must have been developed by a woman to torment and tease and seduce. One whiff of the musky scent, and his hair started to sweat. Another, and he found himself thinking of hot, steamy nights and wild sex. It was enough to push a usually cautious man right over the edge.

He shouldn't have come, he thought, cursing his own stupidity. The last thing he'd wanted was to think of her as a woman, but after tonight he'd never be able to look at her again and see just an inspector. And to make matters worse, she didn't even seem to be aware of what she was doing to him. She hardly spared him a glance, and when her gaze did inadvertently cross his, she only smiled and turned her attention back to the game. He should have been thrilled, at the very least, relieved. Instead he was unreasonably irritated. Calling himself an old fool, he stared determinedly at the screen.

But the lady stubbornly refused to be ignored. "Man, did you see that pick Johnson set?" she suddenly exclaimed. "That guy didn't know what hit him!"

"You ain't whistlin' Dixie, sweetheart," Bill said, hollering enthusiastically with the rest of the crowd in the bar. "He flattened him! Where'd you learn about picks? You play basketball?"

She nodded, chuckling. "Do you even have to ask? I have three brothers who are a head taller than I am and always needed a fourth for an even game."

Bill looked at Roy, who in turn gave Murdock a speaking glance. Already guessing what was coming, Murdock straightened in alarm. "Don't you think we should discuss this?" he began.

But Bill knew a good thing when he saw it. "Now, isn't that interesting," he drawled, deliberately ignoring his friend to give Pru a wide grin. "Sometimes we have the same problem. How good are you?"

Her green eyes sparkled. "I've been told I have a wicked hook shot."

He couldn't have been more delighted if she'd just announced she was Michael Jordan. "I knew there was a reason the angels sent you to us! We play every Sunday in the park, but some of the guys can't always make it and we're a player short. So what do you say? You want to play with us this Sunday? We could really use you."

Surprised, Pru couldn't believe he was serious, but at her side Murdock seemed to be strangling on a curse and the rest of the men were watching her expectantly. She shouldn't, she told herself. But she couldn't resist. Grinning, she nodded. "I'd love to."

Four

For a long moment Murdock didn't say a word. But Pru could practically feel the disapproval rolling off him in waves and knew it was only a matter of time before he told her exactly what he thought of her decision. Glancing at her watch, amusement curling one corner of her mouth, she decided she'd give him ten minutes. Considering the man's short fuse, she should have given him a lot less than that. Seconds later the crowd surrounding them burst into wild cheers as the Spurs' point guard nailed a three-pointer, and that was all the advantage Murdock needed.

"Are you sure you want to do this?" he muttered roughly, leaning over so his words wouldn't carry to the rest of the crew. "Some of the games can get pretty rough. You could get hurt."

Startled, Pru's gaze flew to his, her pulse suddenly galloping in her veins as she found herself reflected in the dark blue depths of his eyes. No man should have eyes that beautiful, she thought inanely. When had he moved so close? His gruff words were like a caress in her ear, his breath so warm and moist on her skin she just wanted to melt against him...which would no doubt horrify him.

Laughing shakily, she murmured teasingly, "Why, Murdock, I'm touched. I didn't know you cared."

"I don't, dammit!" The frustrated words burst from him, and even to his own ears, they sounded like the panicky protests of a man fighting the inevitable. Flushing, he struggled to slap a lid on his temper. "We're not talking about shooting a few baskets in the park. These guys play hard and they play to win. They won't cut you any slack just because you're a woman."

On the TV, the first period ended with a flying dunk by the Spurs' center, bringing most of the crew and the other bar patrons to their feet with a roar. Pru, puzzled by Murdock's warning, never took her eyes from the man at her side. "Is that what you think I expect? Special privileges because I'm usually the only woman in the crowd?"

He wanted to say yes. He would, in fact, have given just about anything to accuse her of being self-centered and pampered and too used to having everything her way or no way. Maybe then he would have been able to dislike her. Maybe then he would have been able to look into those bewitching green eyes of hers and feel nothing but disinterest.

But he couldn't. She might be a pain in the neck on the job, but she knew her onions, had eyes like a hawk, and a real feel for the work. And like it or not, what he felt for her was light-years away from disinterest. And that was what worried him spitless. Lord, she was nearly young enough to be his daughter!

"No," he said finally, quietly. "I just want you to know what you're getting into."

He could have been talking basketball . . . or something else. Her pulse starting to echo in her ears, Pru's eyes searched his, but his gaze was shuttered, telling her nothing. Undaunted, her smile was quick, teasing, confident. "Don't worry. I'm tougher than I look."

She hadn't meant to be provocative, but suddenly his gaze took a lazy tour of the petal-soft texture of her skin, the delicate fragility of her build, the curve of her mouth. When his scorching eyes finally lifted to hers, she could read his thoughts as clearly as if he'd spoken out loud. She might be tough when it came to her job, but he only had to touch her to prove she was soft everywhere he was hard.

Her breathing as ragged as if he'd just stolen a kiss, warm color burning its way up into her cheeks, Pru should have smiled and said something flirty, but her lack of experience in such situations was never more telling and she couldn't think of a thing to say. Then one of the guys asked if anyone wanted anything from the bar and she jumped to her feet, desperate for a few moments to collect herself. "The next round's on me, guys. What'll you have?"

"Beer!" they yelled in unison.

Reluctantly, she glanced at Murdock. "How 'bout you? You want another Bud Light?"

"Yeah." Puzzled, he frowned. "How'd you know I was drinking a light?"

Since she hadn't been there when he'd ordered, Pru didn't have a clue. "I don't know. You just seemed like the kind of guy who would like light beer, medium-rare steaks and your eggs over easy." Grinning at her own imaginings, she headed for the bar and had no idea how her uncannily accurate figuring totally wiped him out. How the hell did she know those things?

After that, there were no more opportunities for one-on-one conversations. She returned with the drinks just as the second period started, and the game quickly grabbed everyone's attention. The Spurs were playing the Phoenix Suns, and both teams were playing hard, physical ball, with neither able to establish any kind of a lead for long.

At her side, Murdock seemed to be as caught up in the game as the others, but she could still feel his eyes on her, studying her as if she were a blueprint he couldn't quite figure out. Pleased, Pru couldn't help but be encouraged. At least he wasn't able to ignore her like he wanted to.

At halftime the score was tied and there was a big discussion of what the Spurs needed to do to pull out a win. Not surprised that she and Murdock shared the same strategy, she couldn't resist needling him. "Don't tell me we actually *agree* on something? Are you feeling all right?"

Unthinkingly, she started to lift a playful hand to his brow to feel for a imaginary fever, but before she ever touched him, his fingers clamped around her wrist. Narrowed blue eyes locked with startled green.

"I feel fine."

The others laughed, drowning out the low rasp of tension in his voice that only she could hear. His grip wasn't tight, but it seemed to set every nerve ending in her arm afire. Her mouth suddenly dry, she licked her lips... and drew a muttered curse from Murdock. He released her abruptly, but not before his grip tightened first.

After that, Pru didn't see much of the rest of the game. The Spurs won, but she couldn't have said how. She only knew she had to leave. Quickly making her excuses, she wished everyone good-night.

"You're leaving?"

Suddenly finding Murdock standing in front of her, she glanced up and wondered if that was disappointment she saw in his eyes. "I only came for the game, and I'm sure the rest of the guys have plans. I'll see you all on Sunday at the park."

She felt his eyes on her all the way to the door, but she didn't look back. If she had, she would have found it impossible to leave. Then the door closed behind her and some of the other patrons who had just come for the game and she stepped out into the night.

Her thoughts on Murdock, it wasn't until she pulled her keys from her purse that she suddenly noticed her left rear tire. It was flat. "Oh, no!"

Muttering curses, she unlocked the driver's door and tossed her purse inside. Her hands planted on her hips, she surveyed the tire in disgust and was stunned to find it as bald as a bowling ball. Damn! When had that happened? She would have sworn her tires were fine.

Glancing at the entrance to the sports bar, she frowned. What was going on here? Was somebody upstairs *trying* to throw her into Murdock's path? First, despite the odds, she'd been permanently assigned to the Fort Sam project so that she had to deal with him every day. And now, when she could have had a flat anywhere, she had one within shouting distance of the man.

A sudden grin tugging at her mouth, she pondered the ironies of fate and wondered what she was supposed to do now. Go back into Charlie's and play the helpless female? One of the guys would surely come to her rescue, and if she was lucky, it would be Murdock.

But even before the idea was fully formed, she dismissed it. She would never pull it off. She was too independent, too capable, too strong to act like a weakling. And she'd never lied worth a damn, she ruefully acknowledged with a quick grin. Her brothers had taught her to change a tire before she'd learned to drive, and if they ever learned she'd even considered playing feminine games, they'd have her hide.

Which meant there was no hope for it, she thought with a sigh of defeat as she stepped around to the rear door and lifted it to retrieve the jack. She would have to change the damn thing herself.

Murdock had planned to stick around for a couple of games of pool, but with Pru gone, he found, much to his annoyance, that he had lost interest. The bar seemed empty without her, the night that stretched ahead endless. Cursing himself for a fanciful old goat, he made his excuses within minutes after she'd left, wanting nothing so much as to be alone and think.

He saw her the minute he stepped outside. She was reaching inside the back of her Jeep, pulling out a jack, the left rear tire of the vehicle as flat as a pancake. No, he thought, jerking to a stop. It couldn't be. Every time he thought he had the problem of Pru Sullivan solved, she popped up again, refusing to be ignored. Almost as if it was fate.

Not liking that train of thought, his blue eyes zeroed in on her slender figure competently setting up the jack. It was obvious she knew what she was doing, and another man might have been able to walk away and leave her to change the tire herself. But not Amanda Murdock's baby boy. It just wasn't in him.

Accepting the inevitable with reluctant, wry humor, he started toward her. "You shouldn't be doing that."

Not seeing him until he was almost upon her, Pru straightened so quickly she almost knocked the jack over on her foot. "Murdock!" Her hand flew to her pounding heart and she laughed shakily. "Lord, I didn't see you. You just took ten years off my life. What are you doing out here?"

"Changing this flat for you before I leave," he replied easily as he stepped around her to lift the spare tire out of the back of the Jeep. "Why didn't you come inside and ask for some help?"

Heat spilled into her cheeks at the thought of how she'd nearly done just that. "Because I can do it myself. I've been changing flats since I was fourteen years old—" She broke off abruptly, her eyes widening at the sight of the spare he set on the ground at her feet. "Oh, no!"

"What—" His gaze following hers, Murdock didn't have to ask what was wrong. The spare was as flat as the flat. "Well, hell."

"I can't believe this! The last time I checked that spare it had plenty of air in it."

"And when was that?"

Thinking back on it, Pru couldn't help but grin. "If I said six months ago, would you think I was a total incompetent?"

Caught in the flash of her dimpled smile, he didn't hear a word she said. Laughter, directed at herself, skimmed over her delicate features, fascinating him. Transfixed, he felt something clench way down deep inside of him and realized with a start of surprise that it was his heart. The knowledge shook him to the core. This couldn't be happening, he thought, grabbing on to denial as if it was a lifeline. She couldn't be getting to him.

But the jackhammer pounding of his heart told him that was exactly what she was doing.

Stunned, he turned away before he did something stupid . . . like reach for her. Grabbing the spare tire instead, he tossed it back into the Jeep, threw in the jack, then slammed the rear door shut. "Any woman who chooses to change a flat herself when she's right outside a whole bar full of men is hardly incompetent," he retorted. "The problem now is finding a garage that's still open at this time of night. Your best bet would probably be to have your car towed to a service station near your apartment, then have the flats fixed in the morning. You can use the car phone in my truck if you like."

It was the logical solution and much more practical than hunting all over town for a garage that was open twenty-four hours. Following Murdock over to his truck, she quickly called a wrecker service, then waited for the tow truck to arrive. It was there within a matter of minutes.

Pru had planned to catch a ride with the tow truck driver to the station where her car would be left, then walk from there to her apartment two blocks away. It wasn't that late, there were still plenty of people out and about, and her neighborhood was a safe one.

But the minute Murdock heard what she intended to do, he looked at her as if she were crazy. "I don't care how safe it is, I'm taking you home."

"But I don't mind walking."

"Then do it in the daytime," he said, pulling open the passenger door of his truck for her. "Not at night, and not alone. There's no use you taking chances when I can drop you off right at your front door."

Normally Pru would have argued with him just because she didn't like accepting favors from anyone for something she was perfectly capable of doing herself. But how could she resist another chance to be alone with him? Her eyes twinkling, she gave in gracefully. "Okay, okay, you win. Let me give the car keys to the tow truck driver and we can go."

He was, Murdock assured himself a few minutes later as she climbed into his truck, just doing her a favor. He would do the same thing for any other woman he found stranded on the side of the road. But as he shut her door for her, then walked around to the driver's side and slipped behind the wheel, it wasn't just any other woman in his truck with him. It was Pru. All five of his senses immediately sprang to full-scale alert.

His eyes on the road, he didn't dare look at her, but he didn't have to. He knew exactly where she sat at her end of the bench seat, not exactly clinging to the door but not hugging the middle, either. Her scent, as subtle as a whisper, called to him, the sweetly spicy essence wafting through the cab of his truck and sliding around him like a lover's arms. His mouth was suddenly as dry as dust, and he swallowed, his blood heating and pooling in dark, secret places of his body.

Finding it nearly impossible to concentrate on his driving, he had to force himself to stare straight ahead at the intersection they were quickly approaching. "Which way?" he grated.

"Left. Then go about a mile and turn right at the stop sign. The Oak Terrace Apartments are halfway down the block on the left. You can't miss it."

Murdock would have given just about anything to ignore her after that, but she made that impossible. Every breath she took echoed in the tense silence, and when they had to stop for red lights—and they hit them all—he could have sworn he heard the pounding of her heart. Time had never seemed so slow.

When the Oak Terrace Apartments finally came into view, all he could think of was dropping Pru off and getting the hell out of there. But as he drove around to the back of the complex, he discovered that her apartment was located in an inner courtyard, so he couldn't let her out right in front of it. Pulling into the closest parking space, he sat there with the motor running, a frown working its way across his brow, his eyes on the complex lighting. Most of it was in the oak trees, creating an attractive, moonlit effect, but the actual illumination it provided wasn't all that much. Between his truck and Pru's front door, there were nothing but pools of dark shadows for her to walk through.

"You don't know how much I appreciate this—"

Making an abrupt decision, Murdock threw the transmission into park and reached for his keys. "I'll walk you to your door."

Surprised, Pru started to sputter, "Oh, b-but you don't have to. I know you want to get home—"

The slamming of his door cut off her wasted protests, and she looked up to find him walking around the front of his truck to open the passenger door for her. Amused, Pru didn't budge. "I think we need to get something straight, Murdock."

He merely lifted a brow. "Oh? And what's that?"

"I'm not some frail, helpless little girl. In fact, in case you hadn't noticed, there's nothing little about me," she said ruefully, casting an amused look at her long legs. "I appreciate your help tonight, but if you hadn't come outside when you had, I would have found a way to handle the problem myself. So you see," she continued, flashing her dimples at him, "I can take care of myself. You don't have to take my hand and show me the way home."

"Fine," he said shortly. "I won't take your hand. But there's no way in hell I'm letting you walk by yourself in the dark all the way to your apartment."

She could have told him that she made that walk by herself every night that she came home late, but his protectiveness felt so good, she couldn't make herself say the words. Suddenly unable to stop smiling, she gave in gracefully. "Okay. If you want to walk in the dark with me, who am I to complain? Let's go."

Her grin flirty, she joined him on the sidewalk and had no idea how close she came to getting herself kissed senseless. Staggered by the unexpected urge to taste her, Murdock couldn't get her home fast enough.

The walk across the complex took only minutes, the sidewalk, for the most part, shrouded in shadows. Murdock didn't touch her, but he hurried her along, not stopping until he reached her front door. Silently standing at her side, he waited for her to unlock the dead bolt and switch the lights on inside.

He was clearly impatient to leave, but Pru just couldn't let him go without a word. Knowing she was pushing her luck, but unable to stop herself, she said softly, "It may not have sounded like it, but I really do appreciate all your help tonight. Thank you." And rising up on tiptoe, she dared to kiss him on the cheek.

The second she started to move, Murdock knew what she was going to do. His hands flew out to stop her, but by the time they settled on her shoulders, it was too late. Her lips, soft and enticing, barely grazed the taut, weathered skin of his cheek, and in the blink of an eye, need slammed into him like a bullet fired without warning in the dark.

Sucking in a sharp breath, he scowled down at her standing in the light that spilled through her open door, his fingers automatically tightening on her shoulders, whether to pull her closer or push her away, he didn't know. And that infuriated him. He couldn't remember the last time he'd been unsure of himself with a woman.

But she wasn't a woman, he tried to convince himself, holding her trapped in front of him. She was little more than a girl to him, a sweet young thing who unwittingly played on a man's deepest vulnerabilities when he suddenly looked up and saw himself bearing down on fifty. And that made her far too dangerous for his peace of mind. Decades ago, his grandfather had made the mistake of thinking he could find his lost youth in a girl half his age, and the family was still talking about it today. He'd be damned if he'd follow in the old man's footsteps.

"You wanted to get something straight," he said tersely. "Well, so do I. Don't get any ideas about me, okay? I'm too old for you and I don't mix business and pleasure. Ever. You got that?"

He expected an argument or, at the very least, an accusation that he'd misunderstood her and a simple kiss of gratitude. But she only smiled faintly and nodded. "Perfectly."

That should have put an end to any fairy tale fantasies she was harboring, but as she stood quietly beneath his hands, she gazed up at him with clear green eyes that were too knowledgeable for one so young, too patient for her generation, which seemed to thrive on instant gratification.

She didn't believe him.

Frustrated, torn between the need to shake her and turn her over his knee, he did neither. Instead he jerked her into his arms and crushed her mouth under his.

He meant to show her that she didn't know beans about kissing or how to handle a man who knew what he was doing. He wasn't going to hurt her—even in his anger, his hands were gentle on her—but he was damn sure going to teach her a lesson or two. Like she was out of her league. Like a man would only take so much sass from a woman before he gave it back to her in triplicate.

But even when he held her this close, the little fool didn't seem to know she was in trouble. What she didn't know about kissing, she was more than willing to let him teach her. And she was a fast learner. Her mouth opened for him, her tongue followed his lead, and suddenly he was reeling as if he'd stepped into quicksand. Familiar. Why did she taste so familiar? And feel so right in his arms? As if he'd been waiting for her, just her, for longer than he could remember?

Rattled, he didn't remember reaching for her hands, but in the next instant he pulled her arms from around his neck and took a long step back. It wasn't far enough. She hadn't made another move toward him, but she didn't have to. Her eyes alone seduced, and he could feel himself being drawn into something he would have sworn he wanted no part of.

"I've got to go," he said abruptly, and turned away. His expression stony, his heart hammering, he stalked back to his truck, fighting the urge to run. So this was what a mid-life crisis felt like, he thought, agitated, as he tore out of the parking lot. All his life he'd heard how Grandpa had gone off the deep end when his hair had started to turn gray, and like everyone else except Grandma, he had laughed. Only now, it wasn't very funny.

Pru spent the night dreaming of Murdock and was still asleep when the doorbell rang at nine in the morning. Half buried under her pillow, she lifted her head only enough to see the clock and moaned. No one she knew would be crazy enough to wake her up on a Saturday morning when it was one of the few days she got to sleep late. Somebody obviously had the wrong apartment.

Burrowing back under the covers, she closed her eyes and sighed, already sliding back into sleep. But whoever was at the door had no intention of being ignored and leaned on the bell. Muttering dire curses, Pru jerked up and reached for her robe.

Her hair was a tangled mass, her green eyes hot as she yanked open the door a few seconds later to find Laura standing on her front step, her grin as bright as the morning sun, looking disgustingly chipper. Pru wanted to shoot her. "Whatever it is, this better be good," she growled.

In answer, Laura held up a white paper bag from Pru's favorite bakery and shook it teasingly under her nose. "I brought double-chocolate-covered doughnuts. Am I forgiven?"

They were her weakness and Laura knew it. "You dog," she laughed. "After waking me, it's the least you can do. Come on in and I'll put on some coffee."

Within minutes they were both seated at the small round table in Pru's kitchen sipping at their coffee, the doughnuts piled on a plate between them. Taking the first bite of the chocolate-covered treat, Pru closed her eyes and just savored the sweetness of it on her tongue. "Mmm. These ought to be outlawed. When I can't fit into my jeans, I'll know who to blame."

Not the least bit worried, Laura licked the chocolate from her fingers, her blue eyes twinkling. "I always did say they were almost as good as sex. So how did last night go?"

Pru almost choked. "Laura!"

"What?" she asked, widening her eyes innocently. "Don't you want to talk about sex and your hot date in the same breath?"

Well used to her friend's outrageousness, Pru only shook her head at her, unable to hold back a smile. "It wasn't a date. And there was no sex!" Remembering the kiss she'd dared to give Murdock and the much, much hotter one he'd given her, faint color stole into her cheeks. "Well," she amended ruefully, "not the kind you're talking about, anyway."

"Oh-ho! So you're holding out on me. Tell me everything."

Her smile fading, she reached for another doughnut. "I gave him a peck on the cheek, and he grabbed me and laid one on me."

"He *kissed* you? An honest-to-God, knee-melting kiss?"

Pru nodded. "Then he warned me not to get any ideas about him."

"And are you?" Laura asked, grinning.

"I'm going to marry him," she announced, then sat back and waited for the explosion. It didn't take long.

"You're going to *what!*"

"I'm going to marry—"

"I heard that part!" Laura exclaimed. "Lord, when you were talking about this yesterday, I didn't realize you meant the big M. Darn it all, Sticks, how can you even be thinking about marrying the guy when you don't even know him? You've spent one evening with him, for God's sake! *One evening!*"

"I know," Pru agreed. "It sounds crazy, doesn't it? Don't ask me how I know it—I can't explain it. I just know every time I look in Zebadiah Murdock's eyes, I know I'm going to marry him. Now all I have to do is convince him."

"Then God help you," Laura said. "Because you're going to need it."

She didn't tell Pru anything she didn't already know. All the rest of that day and half of Sunday morning, she thought of nothing but Murdock and the look in his blue eyes when he'd warned her not to get any ideas about him. He'd been dead serious, and she might have taken him at his word if not for one thing...the expression on his face after he'd kissed her. He'd looked like a man who hadn't known up from down, in from out, right from wrong. He'd wanted to be furious with her, but his eyes had burned with a fire that had nothing to do with temper, a fire that had warmed her all the way to her heart.

Haunted by that heated look, Pru watched the clock draw closer to the time to leave for the Sunday afternoon pickup game and debated with herself over whether she should go or not. She'd originally intended to, but after thinking about it, she was no longer sure that was such a good idea. She would have liked nothing more than to chase him until she caught him, but instinct warned her he was an old-fashioned man who wouldn't appreciate such tactics. If she wanted to get his attention, she would have a better time of it by standing still and letting *him* chase *her*.

Which would have been all well and good if she'd had more than a smidgen of patience. How could she wait for him to make the first move when she felt like she'd already waited an eternity for him?

Troubled, restless, she found a way to distract herself by giving the kitchen stove a thorough cleaning. Whoever had lived in the apartment before her obviously hadn't been bothered by grease, so she had her work cut out for her. Disgusted, she was up to her elbows in soap suds when the phone rang.

Hastily wiping her hands on a dishcloth, she grabbed the phone on the fourth ring and nearly groaned when she recognized Bill Dancer's voice. Why couldn't it have been Murdock? "Hi, Bill. What can I do for you?"

"Are you ready?"

Pru didn't have to ask for what. "Actually, I've decided not to go," she admitted. "You guys don't need me, and I've got some stuff to do around here in the apartment."

"Aw, come on," he protested. "You can't back out now. We need you." When she snorted at that, he said sincerely, "No, really, I'm not kidding. Roy's got some kind of stomach virus so he's not going to be able to play. And a couple of the other guys had plans, so they can't make it, either. If you cancel, too, I don't think we're going to have enough to play."

They could have played shorthanded or even, God forbid, done something else if enough guys didn't show. But after growing up with three brothers who lived and breathed sports, she knew about guys and their games and how grumpy they could get if things didn't work out the way they'd planned. If she didn't go and they ended up not being able to play, she'd never hear the end of it. "Are you sure you can't get anyone else?"

"Not at this late date. We've got to be at the park in twenty minutes."

Lifting her eyes heavenward, she sighed. Somebody up there was pulling strings again, just as Bill was pulling a guilt trip on her. But he—and whoever was in charge upstairs—was also giving her another legitimate excuse to see Murdock away from work, and she couldn't resist. "All right, I'll go. But I don't know if I can be there in twenty minutes. I've got to change and then find the place—"

"I'll pick you up," he cut in quickly. "That'll save time. See you in ten minutes." Not giving her a chance to protest, he hung up.

Watching the scene with a frown of consternation, Joshua glanced at St. Peter and arched a brow. "Uh, sir, I haven't said anything before, but I'm confused. I thought we weren't supposed to interfere."

"We're not."

"But Prudence's tire—and spare—didn't go flat by themselves, did they? And what about Roy Wilkins? He's sick and he hasn't missed a day of work in five years."

St. Peter nodded sagely. "A dedicated man. The world needs more like him."

More confused than ever, Joshua blinked. "Are you saying all those things were coincidence?"

His smile secretive, St. Peter shrugged. "Maybe. Maybe not."

Five

Waiting for the others to arrive, Murdock absently shot some baskets to warm up, his mind, as it had for days now, wandering to Pru. If she had any sense, she wouldn't show. She might know basketball and even be a pretty good shooter, but she would never be able to hold her own as the only woman in a group of men. She was too short, too delicate. And they played rough. They might rib her tomorrow at work for chickening out, but that was better than getting knocked around by a bunch of guys who outweighed her by a good forty or fifty pounds.

It was, he decided, for the best. The lady had felt too good at his side the other night at Charlie's. And then there was the matter of a kiss he didn't want to think about.

His mouth grim, he told himself it was just a damn kiss. No different than the ones he'd given dozens of women over the years. He should have put it out of his head the moment he'd walked away. But from the first moment he'd had the misfortune to tangle with Pru Sullivan on the phone, nothing had gone as it should. He couldn't get her out of his thoughts, couldn't forget the feel of her warm, hungry mouth under his. For two nights now, he'd brooded over it, dreamed of it. And ached. For a girl who was young enough to be his daughter.

Just like Grandpa.

God, he groaned silently. It was in the genes.

Several car doors slammed then, the sound dragging him back to his surroundings, and he glanced up to see some of his workers spilling out of the pickups that he hadn't even heard drive up. He started to smile, only to freeze, his gaze locked on the woman who stepped out of a truck that had just pulled up at the curb.

Pru.

If he'd looked past her to the black Ford she'd arrived in, he would have recognized it immediately, but for a long, timeless moment he saw nothing but her. Looking like a teenager with her hair pulled back into a ponytail and her face free of makeup, she was dressed just like the men in T-shirt, shorts and leather Nikes. But that was where the resemblance ended.

Her blue-and-white knit top was loose-fitting and comfortable, but if she'd hoped to conceal her femininity, she'd failed miserably. Any man with eyes could see the curve of her breasts outlined by the soft folds of material. And she damn sure shouldn't have worn those shorts if she'd wanted to blend into the crowd. Red-hot in color, they weren't particularly tight or even all that short, but they emphasized every sweet, beautiful inch of the longest, prettiest legs he'd ever seen.

His blood heated and thickened in his veins, and without realizing what he was doing, he took a step toward her... only to stop at the sight of Bill alighting from the same pickup Pru had just stepped from. It was only then that the realization his eyes had already noted hit him. She'd come with Bill.

He swore and didn't have a clue what he said, a fury he hadn't expected punching him right in the stomach. So she was with one of his best friends, he thought savagely. What the hell did he care? He didn't want her there, period. If she wanted to start seeing a married man, that was her business. He just wished like hell she wouldn't do it in front of him.

Turning his back on her, he said tersely, "It looks like everybody's here that's coming. Let's get started and choose up sides—shirts and no shirts." Jerking off his own shirt, he chose his team without saying a word. Since Pru could hardly do the same thing, they were automatically on different teams, which was more than all right with him. After all, they'd been squaring off from the moment they'd met and *that* was a relationship he was comfortable with.

It took him all of ten seconds to realize he'd made a drastic mistake. Instead of playing with her, he found himself in the unexpectedly erotic position of defending against her. Tall for a woman, she was the smallest player on either team, but she was quick as lightning and a damn good basketball player. Going after a loose ball, she brushed against him, grabbed the ball, and shot around him to score before he could do anything but suck in a sharp breath.

"Yeah!"

"Way to go, Pru!"

"Hey, guys, we got us a winner here. Let's kick some butt!"

His pulse throbbing stronger than it should have considering the game had just started, Murdock watched the shirts team rally around Pru and slap high-fives with her, and it was all he could do not to grind his teeth in irritation. Letting her past him was his mistake and everyone knew it. Scowling, he sternly ordered himself to concentrate.

Determined to be prepared for the brush of her body against his the next time the game brought them together, he took the ball, only to suddenly find himself guarded by Pru. The very idea of her trying to stop him from scoring was laughable. All he had to do was shoot over her head.

But before he could take the shot, she was right in front of him, her fingers sliding across his as she tried to steal the ball. Heat, like a hot wind that suddenly came out of nowhere, whispered across his skin from his fingertips all the way to his shoulder. Surprised, his grip on the ball eased for just a second. That was all Pru needed to steal it.

She heard him curse as he made a grab for her, but laughing, she managed to elude him, take two steps, then go straight up into the air and shoot. With a swoosh, the ball fell through the hoop, catching nothing but net.

"Son of a . . . gun!"

Pru giggled, her eyes dancing, but there was no time to enjoy the small victory. In the blink of an eye, Murdock had taken the ball, stepped out of bounds and thrown it back to one of his teammates. The game was on.

Holding her own with the men, Pru threw herself into the competition, silently sending up a prayer of thanks for the valuable lessons she'd learned from her brothers years ago. But it was Murdock's reaction to her that really elated her. She was getting to him. Oh, he hid it very well, but she saw the way his eyes burned every time the momentum of the game brought their bodies into contact. Who would have thought it? Zebadiah Murdock rattled...by her.

It didn't take an Einstein to see that he wanted to throttle her. Her dimples flashing, she remembered the way he had turned his back on her when she'd arrived, the hurt that simple act had sent streaking through her like snake venom. So he thought he could ignore her, did he? Let him try.

Sweating, her T-shirt damp and clinging, her hair pulling from its ponytail, she stood at midcourt and dribbled the ball, her smile provocative in a way that would have shocked her last week as her sparkling eyes met Murdock's. He stood right in front of her, blocking her way to the basket, just daring her to try to get past him.

She could have thrown the ball to one of her teammates. Bill was open and within three feet of the basket. But one look at Murdock's narrowed eyes and she knew that was just what he expected her to do. Her heart thumping, she decided that it was time that Murdock learned she seldom did what was expected.

Murdock couldn't believe it when she came right at him, waiting until the last second to dart around him to drive right down the middle of the lane. Little witch! Did she really think he was just going to stand there and let her fly past him? Forgetting there was anyone else on the court but the two of them, his only thought to stop her, he swore and threw himself in front of her.

Frustrated, his blood pumping, he grunted as she plowed into him, the force of the collision staggering them both. Cursing, he felt her start to fall and automatically snatched her close and wrapped his arms around her, but her slight weight, combined with their momentum, was too much for him. With a string of curses, they went down in a tangle of arms and legs.

They hit the asphalt pavement of the outdoor court hard. His breath tearing through his lungs, Murdock managed to twist his body at the last minute so that Pru landed on him, instead of the rough ground, but it still hurt. Winded, his blood roaring in his ears, he felt the soft curves of her breasts against his chest, the thundering of her heart, and looked up to find her mouth only inches from his. With a will of their own, his arms tightened around her, dragging her close.

Somewhere in the back of his mind, he was aware of the shouts of alarm from the rest of the men, the quick, worried questions thrown at them as everyone rushed forward to help, but they might as well have been on another planet for all the attention he took of them. This close, he couldn't see anything but the wide, bottomless depths of Pru's sea green eyes.

Lord, she was beautiful. No woman had a right to look so gorgeous after a hard game of basketball. She was hot and sweaty and so damn soft in his arms he wondered how he could possibly let her go anytime soon.

"Are you all right?" he asked, his voice a low rumble.

She nodded, the loosened clasp in her hair giving way completely so that her chestnut curls spilled forward like a curtain around her face. No one but Murdock saw her lick her suddenly dry lips. And no one but Pru heard—or felt—the nearly silent groan that rippled through him. Her eyes locking with his, she went perfectly still above him.

He could have held her like that forever, but the world just wouldn't go away. Before he was ready to release her, Bill and some of the others were hunkering down around them, reaching to help them both up.

"You guys okay?"

"That was quite a spill you took."

"Wow, girl, you really did a number on that knee of yours," Bill said gruffly, frowning down at her leg. "That's got to sting like the devil."

It did, in fact, burn like the flames of Hell, but Pru only gingerly accepted the hands outstretched to lift her to her feet, then bent down to brush herself off. "It's nothing. Just a scrape."

"The hell it is!" Murdock snapped. "You're bleeding."

He sounded so horrified, Pru had to smile. "Just a little. It's nothing that a little soap and water won't clean up."

But when one of the men wet a handkerchief at the water fountain for her to clean the wound, blood continued to seep down her leg. Sick at the thought of hurting her, Murdock had to force himself to keep his distance. "You'd better take her home, Bill," he said curtly, "so she can get a bandage on that. It looks pretty nasty."

"It's no big deal—"

Ignoring her protests, Bill frowned down at her. "You think you can walk to the truck? It's not that far."

"Of course I can walk. I didn't break my leg or anything. It's just a little blood. Come on, guys, we can't stop now," she cried. "The game's tied!"

At any other time, there was no way in hell they would have walked away from a tie ball game, but Murdock wasn't the only one who had lost his taste for the game after seeing Pru's blood. Mumbling excuses, the others started toward the parking lot and Pru was left with no choice but to gingerly head for Bill's truck.

The last to leave, Murdock stood alone on the court and watched Bill's black pickup disappear from view around the corner, the image of the way the other man had helped Pru into his truck playing over and over again in his head. Steeling himself against the green envy that curled in his stomach like billowing hot smoke, he tried to convince himself he didn't care. If Pru wanted to see Bill and every member of his crew, that was her business and he didn't give a damn.

It sounded good, but inside his head, a little voice that refused to be ignored taunted softly, *Sure you don't. Then why do you feel like you want to hit something?*

Muttering a curse, he grabbed the basketball and dribbled down the court, launching himself into the air nearly six feet away from the basket to deliver a rim-rattling slam dunk. Seconds later he raced past the three-point line, turned abruptly, and threw up a quick shot that banged off the front of the rim. Chasing the ball down, he caught it before it rolled into the street, then sprinted back to the court to start all over again.

For thirty minutes he played one-on-one against the demons of a jealousy he wanted no part of. Driven, he pushed himself like a man possessed. It didn't help. By the time he finally called it quits and climbed into his truck, he felt every one of his nearly forty-five years. And Pru was still as firmly lodged in his thoughts as if she'd always been a part of him.

Disgusted, he went home to the rundown old carriage house he'd bought three months ago in the King William area of the city, a neighborhood of Victorian homes that had been built in the shadow of downtown at the turn of the century. He was restoring the place himself and had spent the past week stripping the beautiful walnut wainscotting some idiot had covered with white lead paint more than half a century ago. Only taking time to change into jeans and an old T-shirt, he set to work.

It was a tedious task that couldn't be rushed, one that required all his concentration. The wood was old and beautiful and his only thought was not to damage it any more than it had been already. Time blurred, and outside the last of the daylight faded into darkness. One by one the stars came out, and just that easily Pru slipped back into his thoughts.

At first, he hardly noticed. Her image drifted through his consciousness, then was gone as quickly as a dream that faded upon waking. His eyes focused on his hands, he carefully worked a putty knife through the bubbled paint that he'd applied paint remover to a few minutes earlier. Half finished with one wall of the entrance hall, he drew back to survey his handiwork and suddenly found himself wondering what Pru's reaction would be to the place when she saw it.

Not if, but *when.*

The notion literally set him back on his heels. When had he started thinking about bringing her here?

Before he could deal with the answer to that, the phone in his study rang. Thankful for the distraction, he pushed to his feet and groaned as the muscles of his back protested that he'd been at the task too long without a break. Making his way to the study, he snatched up the phone. "Murdock."

"Mr. Murdock, this is Lieutenant Barker," the caller identified himself. "I'm an M.P. at Fort Sam."

Murdock's fingers tightened around the receiver, foreboding sliding like an icy hand around his throat. "I'm familiar with your name, Lieutenant. Is there a problem at the site?"

"Yes, sir, I'm afraid there is. It's been vandalized, and a suspect was able to get away before we could apprehend him. I think you'd better come, sir."

His mouth compressed into a flat line, Murdock was already reaching for his keys. "I'll be right there."

On a good day Murdock usually made it to the site in fifteen minutes. That night the trip took him eight and a half. Running every yellow light and rolling through some of the red ones, he braked sharply next to his office and pushed the driver's side door open before his truck had shuddered to a complete stop.

He saw in a glance that the M.P.'s had surrounded the site, the light bars of their vehicles throwing a flashing red, white and blue glow over everything. The lieutenant hadn't given him any details, so Murdock had no idea what to expect. Stepping from his truck, his eyes quickly searched for the damage.

He didn't have to look far to find it. The chain-link fence that he'd had constructed on Friday was down, a twisted tangle that had probably been flattened by whatever vehicle the vandal had been driving. And not surprisingly, considering the gaping opening in the fence, the dogs were nowhere in sight. The rest of the site looked relatively normal, but Murdock knew better than to trust first impressions.

Just then one of the M.P.'s walked out of the partially completed entrance foyer of the communications building. Spying Murdock, he hurried forward, his expression somber, the nameplate on his uniform identifying him as Barker. "Mr. Murdock? Glad you could get here so fast. From what I can tell, the damage seems to be limited to the plumbing. The vandal poured concrete down every open drain and pipe he could find—"

Murdock swore. "Is it still wet?"

"Yes, sir, but it's hardening pretty quick."

"Then we don't have any time to waste." Pulling out his keys, he quickly unlocked his office and snatched up the phone to call Roy. In a few short sentences, he explained the situation. "Round up some of the other men and get over here as soon as you can." Hanging up, he turned back to the lieutenant. "Can you spare some of your men until my crew gets here? I could use your help."

The younger man could have turned him down. His job was security, and the longer he waited to follow up on the few clues the vandal had left, the harder it would be to catch him. But he was already reaching for his walkie-talkie. "Let me call for backup to secure the area, and the rest of us will do what we can."

The damage turned out to be worse, much worse, than Murdock had expected. With a viciousness that infuriated Murdock, the vandal had filled every open pipe and drain to overflowing with thick, wet cement that was already starting to harden in the warm night air. Shouting orders to the M.P.'s, he flew into action to control the damage. Dragging out water hoses and powerful shop vacuums, he started with the east wing.

If the pipes couldn't be saved, he didn't even want to think about the weeks of work that would have to be torn out to replace them.

"Find a hydrant that's working," he told the lieutenant, shoving the hose into his arms. "If we're lucky, we might be able to flush some of the softer stuff right down the drain." Turning to the rest of the M.P.'s, he said, "See if you can suck the cement out with the shop vacuums. And don't worry about ruining the damn things. They're a lot cheaper to replace than the pipes."

A slow-burning anger glowing like a fireball in his gut, he grabbed some trowels, dropped to his knees, and started digging the concrete out of one of the larger drain openings by hand. It was a frustrating job, and by the time Roy and half the crew arrived, he was up to his elbows in the thick mess.

He was fighting a losing battle. He and every man there knew it. But defeat was something he had never accepted easily, and he'd be damned if he'd let some bastard of a vandal destroy something he'd spent more than a month of backbreaking work building.

Pru saw what remained of the fence the second she arrived at the site the next morning. She paled, her heart starting to thump, her eyes searching as she surveyed the rest of the project. Except for the fence, everything else looked perfectly normal. The crew was already busily at work, the normal sounds of construction ringing in the early morning air. But something was wrong. She could feel it.

"Roy!" Seeing him heading for the west wing, she rushed over to intercept him. "Was there more vandalism last night? The fence—"

"I know," he said wearily, rubbing the back of his neck. "Somebody knocked it down before midnight and poured cement down the pipes."

"Oh, no!"

"Yeah, it's been a bitch. We came in last night for about four hours, but there wasn't a hell of a lot we could do once the junk started to dry."

With just a few words, he painted an image in her mind of the men frantically working against the clock in the middle of the night. And with hardly any rest at all, they were back at work with a full day stretching ahead of them. Dear Lord, they had to be exhausted!

"Did anyone see anything?" At the shake of his head, she gasped indignantly. "But how can this happen? This is a U.S. Army base, for God's sake! How can someone just knock down a fence and trash the place without anyone seeing anything? The M.P.'s—"

"Were tied up on the other side of the quadrangle with a three-car accident," he replied. "Two of the drivers were drunk and got into a fight, and by the time they were taken care of, the damage was done."

"Murdock must be furious."

For the first time Roy's usual good humor peaked out of his eyes. "Let's put it this way. For a while there last night, you could see the steam coming out of his ears."

Considering the circumstances, Pru couldn't blame him. Suddenly needing to see him, she glanced around, but he was nowhere in sight. "Where is he?"

"In his office. But I don't know if you want to go in there. He's still pretty hot."

That was no doubt a whopper of an understatement, but Pru only said, "Thanks for the warning," and headed for the small portable building at the edge of the building site.

She knocked, but didn't wait for an invitation to enter, half afraid she was the last person Murdock wanted to see. Something had passed between them yesterday, something that had had her rearranging her kitchen cabinets at two in the morning. Something that wasn't going to be assuaged with a kiss or two. An inevitability that she'd seen in his eyes, felt in his touch, when they'd fallen on the court.

Her heart pounding, she pulled open the door and stepped inside to find him sitting at his desk filling out paperwork, no doubt for the insurance company. The second he glanced up at her entrance, they were both transported back to yesterday.

Her heart contracted at the sight of him, but he only nodded and immediately returned his attention to the report he was making. With his face shadowed with a night's growth of beard and carved with lines that hadn't been there yesterday, he looked tired. Bone-weary, eye-burning exhausted. Her own eyes suddenly hot with tears, she blinked rapidly before he could see how much she hurt for him.

"Roy told me what happened," she said, breaking the silence. "You've been here all night, haven't you?"

He shrugged, not glancing up. "With the fence down, someone had to stay. I couldn't take a chance on any more damage."

His tone was matter-of-fact, no nonsense, controlled. But with a certainty she no longer questioned, Pru knew he wasn't nearly as calm as he appeared on the surface. Barely checked rage was clearly seen in every tense line of his body.

Too late, she realized that now was probably not the best time to approach him. But it tore at her heart to see him dealing with this all by himself. Daring to draw his wrath, she sank into the chair angled in front of his desk. That brought his head, his blue eyes sharp as a hawk's, snaring hers.

He should have known it took more than a killer look from him to make her squirm. Not the least impressed, she didn't even flinch. "I know this is none of my business, but I'm going to stick my nose into it, anyway. Something's going on here, something that has nothing to do with mistakes in supply orders or even just plain bad luck. And I want to know what it is."

"Why? So you can run to your boss with it?"

That hurt. Her gaze reproachful, she asked, "Do you really think I'd do something like that?"

A week ago he would have said yes in a heartbeat. But try though he might, he could no longer think of her as just an inspector whose sole purpose in life was to make his miserable. He trusted her and he didn't even know how it had happened.

"No," he said huskily. "Just forget I said that. It was a hell of a night."

She didn't have to explain herself, but she did. "If I've been a pain in the butt, it's only because my boss is just looking for an excuse to fire me. He doesn't like women inspectors any more than you do."

The little gibe brought a reluctant smile to his lips and, as she'd hoped, took his mind of the vandalism for a second. "I never said I didn't like women inspectors. I don't like inspectors, period. Sex has nothing to do with it."

"And here I thought it was just me." He grinned, but then his eyes fell on his report and his smile vanished. Wishing she could get her hands on whoever had done this to him, she demanded, "Who would do this? It's got to be personal—it's too vicious. Who has that kind of grudge against you?''

Murdock could think of a whole list of people who might fit that description, and suddenly he was sick of the games, the politics, the dog-eat-dog world of government contracts. "It could be anyone," he said tiredly, clearly surprising her with the admission as he set his pen down abruptly and leaned back tiredly in his chair. "But if I had to give an educated guess, I'd say it was one of my competitors and someone in the crew."

Pru couldn't have been more shocked if he'd just announced he'd vandalized the place himself to collect on the insurance. "You can't be serious!"

But he was. Never more so. And it was tearing him apart. His crew was hand-picked, comprised of men he'd worked with for years and trusted like family. He'd fought it for as long as he could afford to, but he could no longer avoid what was slapping him right in the face. All the facts pointed to a traitor in his midst, someone who was doing his damnedest to destroy him and the project.

A muscle working in his clenched jaw, he struggled to put a lid on the rage boiling up inside him like a geyser. "I bid this job lower than dirt and made a lot of enemies in the process. If someone wanted to get me fired, it wouldn't be all that difficult if they could find a weak spot in my crew. Some money passes hands and suddenly problems start cropping up. Before you know it, I'm behind schedule and over budget and unable to finish the job when money gets tight. And every other builder in town is standing in the wings, just waiting to take over when I'm fired."

It was a cynical viewpoint but, Pru knew, a realistic one, considering how much money there was to be made in the cutthroat world of government contracts. But, Lord, her heart ached for him. She'd watched him with his crew; they were all friends. Or at least all but one of them was.

Sick at the thought, her eyes met his. "You know your crew better than anyone else. Who would take money to betray you?"

"I don't know," he said flatly. "Tommy Walker has been known to drink up his check on a weekend. Victor Jimenez likes to play the horses at Bandera Downs. And Steven Gonzalez is raising his brother's three kids. Hell, if you think about it, I guess any one of them could use some extra money. Nobody ever makes enough."

Frustrated, the rage he could no longer control finally exploding in him, he cursed and shot to his feet, knocking his chair back into the wall. "Whoever the bastard is, he's stabbed me in the back for the last time! I'm going to put an end to this garbage right now." Striding over to the filing cabinet crammed into the corner, he jerked open the top drawer and pulled out a pistol.

Pru gasped. "My God, Murdock, have you lost your mind? Put that away!"

Ignoring her, he strapped the weapon on, his face stony. When he turned toward Pru, she was standing between him and the door. "Get out of my way, Pru. This is my problem and I'm going to solve it my way."

"How?" she demanded. "By getting yourself arrested? You know only M.P.'s are allowed to have weapons on base."

"If they want to arrest someone, let them arrest the jackass who trashed this place last night. Now get out of my way."

He was pushed to the edge, spoiling for a fight, his chiseled face carved in harsh lines. A wise woman would have cut a wide path around him and steered clear of him until he'd had a chance to cool off. But instead of moving away from him, Pru backed up until she felt the door against her back. Her heart in her throat, she said hoarsely, "No. You're not thinking straight. If you'd just listen to me—"

But he wasn't going to. She could see the decision in his eyes as he started toward her with grim determination. He'd made up his mind and nothing she could say was going to change it. Like a tiger stalking a mouse, he towered over her threateningly, his hands reaching for her to move her out of the way.

Desperate, horribly afraid he was going to do something stupid if she didn't find a way to stop him, she did the only thing she could think of to get his attention. She stood on tiptoe, wrapped her arms around his neck, and kissed him.

Six

She'd thought it would be easy. He might deny it until the cows came home, but he was as drawn to her as she was to him, and seducing him out of his nasty temper should have been as simple as kissing him. But at her first touch, he stiffened, his hands clamping at her waist to push her away. Desperate to stop him, she clung tighter, her hands clutching, her mouth frantic as she kissed him again and again. "Don't," she cried softly against his hard, unyielding lips. "Please, Zeb, don't do this."

Murdock froze at the sound of his Christian name on her tongue, the sane, rational part of his brain that wasn't overcome by fury staggered by the feel of her against him. Damn her daring. What the hell did she think she was doing? He wasn't some inexperienced kid at the mercy of his own hormones; it took a hell of a lot more than a kiss to distract him when he was in a rage.

Or at least, that was what he tried to tell himself. But while his mind might be caught up in the red-hot heat of anger, his body was concentrating on something altogether different. Like the tantalizing fullness of her breasts pressed to his chest and the irresistible temptation of her hips and thighs nudging his. Just like the siren who had trespassed in his dreams night after night for the past week, she seduced with nothing more than her nearness.

He should have pushed her away then. His fingers were already tightening on her waist to do so, but she never gave him the chance. As if she sensed his intentions, the desperate pressure of her mouth against his suddenly softened. Murmuring his name, she melted against him, her tongue gliding along his bottom lip, teasing, cajoling, seducing.

She kissed like a woman who had been alone too long, lonely too long, like his taste was something new and heady, something to be savored. As if *he* was something to be savored, he thought with a low groan. And suddenly the heat fogging his brain had nothing to do with anger and everything to do with the woman in his arms. Dazed, he realized he'd released her waist, but only to pull her close until she was flush against him. She fit him perfectly, as if she'd been made just for him by someone who'd known his every dream and fantasy. And her mouth. Lord, the woman had a sweet mouth. She lit a candle in his blood, and he could no more resist returning her kiss than a wolf could resist the call of the wild. Not knowing if he murmured her name or a curse, he slanted his mouth across hers and gave himself to the desire he'd been fighting from the moment he'd first laid eyes on her.

When he was finally forced to let her up for air, they were both breathless, their lungs straining. For what seemed like an eternity, they just stared at each other in stunned surprise, neither able to move.

His mind spinning, Murdock had no idea how long he stood there before it suddenly hit him that he was gazing at her like a grizzly old recluse who hadn't seen a woman in years and now suddenly found himself in a harem. Which was just how he felt. He couldn't remember the last time he had wanted a woman who was so wrong for him so quickly or quite so badly. God, he burned.

He set her from him abruptly, knowing if he didn't then, he never would. "I don't know what you think you're doing, but I suggest you don't try that again."

Shaken, electricity still sparking along her nerve endings, she winced at his harsh tone. "Why?" she dared ask, stung. "Because you liked it more than you wanted to?"

He'd have given just about anything to deny it, but she'd been on the receiving end of that kiss, and she knew as well as he did that he'd more than liked the feel of her in his arms. He'd damn near gone up in flames.

Scowling at her, he demanded, "Just how old are you?"

Surprised by the sudden change in subject, she blinked. "Twenty-eight. Why?"

"Because you're just a baby compared to me, sweetheart. I'll be forty-five next July. I was dating before you were born, so if you're looking for a man, go find somebody else. I'm too old for you."

The words hurt, but not as much as they might have if Pru hadn't been watching his eyes. Resentful, frustrated, they spoke of a need that burned hotter than the hottest fire.

Wanting to touch him, reluctantly accepting that now was not the time, she lifted her chin, her green eyes daring. "With another kiss or two, I could prove you wrong about that, but that's not why I kissed you. I didn't kiss you because I'm looking for a man. I was trying to distract you so you wouldn't rush out of here like a bat out of hell and blow somebody's head off with that stupid thing." She nodded distastefully at the gun strapped to his hip. "And it worked."

What worked was all his vital parts, he thought grimly. Disgusted with himself, he reached out suddenly and took her by the shoulders, moving her out of the way before she could stop him. "Only because you caught me off guard," he retorted. Grabbing his hard hat, he jammed it on his head and pushed open his office door.

"Damn you, Zeb!" she cried, hurrying after him. "This isn't going to solve anything."

If he heard her, he ignored her. His long legs quickly outdistancing hers, he strode to the middle of the construction compound and whistled at Roy to round up the men. Within minutes, word had spread through the various buildings of the site and he was surrounded by his men.

Edging her way through the crowd of construction workers until she reached the middle of the wide circle they'd formed around him, Pru stood on trembling legs, her heart in her throat. Behind her, she could hear the men murmuring to each other, speculating that the meeting had been called to discuss the vandalism of the previous night. She knew to a second when they spotted the sidearm strapped to Murdock's hip. Shocked silence rippled through the morning air.

Her gut knotting with apprehension, she stared unblinkingly at Murdock where he stood all alone, looking taller than ever with his yellow hard hat on his head, surrounded by men he considered friends. Somewhere in the crowd was a snake in the grass. Pru knew the knowledge had to be eating at him like a cancer, but his face was expressionless, almost frighteningly composed. And the gun was still at his side.

Desperately sending up a silent prayer for help, Pru stared at him unblinkingly, willing him to look at her, to give her one more chance to talk him out of this madness. But he stubbornly refused to make eye contact with her even though she was sure he knew she was there, standing on the edge of the crowd.

"I'm sure you're all wondering why I called you together this morning," he said suddenly, breaking the eerie silence that had settled over the construction site that was usually ringing with noise. "I felt it was time we had a talk."

His tone was cool and even, but his men weren't fooled. Feet shuffled in the dirt, and somewhere in the back of the crowd someone mumbled, "Oh, hell, I don't like the sound of this."

Ignoring that remark, he continued in a voice that had grown noticeably colder. "I don't have to tell you about all the problems we've been having around here. You know about the stolen tools and disappearing materials...and last night's vandalism." His jaw rock-hard, he glanced around, his eyes seeming to search out one nameless face in the crowd. "What you don't know is that there's a good possibility that the person responsible for all this isn't just some thug off the street. In fact, I have good reason to believe it's one of the crew."

"*What?*"

"Son of a bitch!"

"One of us? Like hell!"

The shocked explosions were immediate, starting at a murmur and accelerating to a roar of outrage. Undaunted, Murdock didn't so much as blink. "You know I made some enemies when I got the bid on this job, enemies who would love to see me fall on my face. And what better way to do it than to get to one of my men. That's right," he said harshly, raising his voice so that he easily overpowered the angry mutterings. "He might be one of us, and I'll tell you one thing... it turns my stomach to know that someone we've all trusted might be stabbing us in the back. And it's going to stop. You hear me? Whoever's doing this, you'd better listen and listen good. Because I've had all of this crap I'm going to take. The M.P.'s haven't been able to do much, so I'll see what I can do to put an end to it. And I guarantee you won't like my methods." And just in case they didn't all get the message, he patted the gun at his hip suggestively.

For a startled moment there was nothing but dead silence. Then Victor Jimenez swore and threw his hard hat on the ground at Murdock's feet. "You're a crazy son of a bitch, Murdock, if you think I'm going to stand here and let you threaten me. I don't care if you are a friend, I don't take that kind of garbage from anyone. I quit!"

"Me, too," Larry Archer, another independent contractor, said, pitching his hard hat down next to Victor's. "If you don't know me well enough to know that you can trust me, then I don't want to work for you. Find yourself another mud man."

He stalked off, pushing his way through the tense, increasingly hostile crew. Murdock didn't so much as flinch. His eyes piercing, he glanced around at the men still watching him warily. "If anyone else wants to speak their piece, this is the time."

No one had the guts to say anything, but before the dust had settled, Sean Nelson and Jerome Bishop, two carpenters, had also walked off the job, probably never to return. Watching them as they collected their gear, Murdock would have liked to believe that one of the four had quit because he was guilty as hell and afraid of getting caught. But they had seemed genuinely outraged by his daring to face them with a gun strapped to his hip, and he couldn't doubt their sincerity.

Which meant, in all likelihood, that he still had a traitor on his payroll. His expression rigid, he said, "Then whichever one of you is guilty, consider yourself forewarned. Now let's get back to work. We've got a hell of a lot of pipe to replace."

Pushing his way through the crowd without another word, he left behind a silence that was tense, suspicious and, in some cases, downright resentful. Suddenly chilled, Pru had to hug herself to keep from going after him. He might have fooled his men into thinking he was every bit as cold and tough as Dirty Harry, but she'd seen the disillusionment hiding behind the anger in his eyes, the hurt he was too proud to admit to. Distrusting men he had always thought of as friends was ripping his heart out, and all she could think about was going to him, hugging him, holding him until the pain went away. But he was still wary of her, so she kept her distance. For now.

* * *

The rest of the day passed with agonizing slowness. The crew went back to work without a word, but the mood was nothing like it had been previously at the site. There was no laughter during breaks, no good-natured kidding or even easy-going conversations between the men in passing. With a tension that was almost palpable permeating every corner of the construction site, Pru had never seen so many grim faces in her life.

Exhausted by the grim atmosphere and the energy it took to act as if nothing was wrong, she felt as if she'd been through a war by the time she finally walked through the front door of her apartment late that afternoon. The muscles at the back of her neck were stiff and knotted, and for the past three hours, a little man had sat in her head and pounded gleefully at her temples until she was nauseated with the pain.

Deliberately forcing the events of the day from her thoughts, she made her way to the bathroom, stripping off her clothes as she went, and stepped into the shower. Her eyes closed, the water thundering down on the tight muscles of her neck and back, she stood under the hot spray until the air was thick with mist and her bones had melted one by one.

By the time she walked into her kitchen twenty minutes later, she felt like a new woman. Her headache was gone and her stomach was clamoring for supper. Opening a can of soup, she made herself a sandwich and sat down at her small kitchen table to eat. In the silence of her own company, Zeb and a kiss that she'd kept locked away in her heart all day slipped into her thoughts.

She'd never been so bold in her life. Never known a man she'd wanted to be so bold with. And she couldn't

regret it. Warmth seeped through her at the memory of
the way he'd groaned and wrapped her close against the
long, hard length of him. From the moment she'd first
laid eyes on him, she'd known he was the man for her,
and like a complete innocent, she'd thought she'd
known what to expect. But it had only taken a couple
of kisses to prove she didn't know squat.

Heaven. Every time he held her close was like heaven,
she thought in growing wonder. He stirred feelings in
her that she'd never thought to feel this side of the
pearly gates. Feelings like the joy of coming home, of
being lost, then found, of discovering a soul-deep inner peace in the last place in this world she'd ever
thought to find it. It was wonderful, fantastic, frightening in its intensity.

And Zeb had felt it, too. Oh, he would die before he
admitted it, but she'd been too close for him to hide the
sudden surge of breath-stealing emotions that had
sneaked up behind him and caught him unaware. He'd
fought it, but for a few precious moments he'd been as
caught up in the wonder and inevitability as she. The
world had faded into a hazy mist and, together at last,
neither of them had had the strength to care.

Her supper forgotten, longing squeezed her heart,
loneliness creeping like a dark, heavy fog through her
apartment. She'd never been uncomfortable with the
silence of her own company, but it got to her now, the
absolute emptiness of her surroundings ringing in her
ears. Blinking back tears, she considered calling her
mother or Laura, but deep down inside, she knew that
wouldn't help. The loneliness would only return the
minute she hung up, and the one person she really
needed right then was halfway across town. Sighing, she
wandered into the living room and switched on the TV.

She'd blindly watched two quarters of "Monday Night Football" and couldn't have said who was even playing when the phone rang. Welcoming the distraction, *any* distraction, she reached for it without getting up from the couch. "Hello?"

"Hi. Am I interrupting anything?"

At the sound of the low murmur in her ear, she almost dropped the phone. "Zeb?"

Not surprised that he'd shocked the hell out of her—he still couldn't believe he'd called her—he couldn't hold back a grin. "Do you know you're the only person on earth that I let get by with that?"

"Get by with what?" she teased. "Calling you Zeb? What about your family?"

"That's different. My ninety-year-old granny does anything she wants."

Delighted, Pru chuckled. "So do I."

The warmth of her soft laughter seeping through him, Murdock was just now beginning to figure that out for himself. "I guess you're wondering why I called."

"Well, I ... Is something wrong?"

Leaning back in his office chair and propping his booted feet on his desk, Murdock marveled that she even had to ask. *Wrong?* Hell, yes, something was wrong! He'd decided to spend the night at the site until the vandal was caught, but the minute his office door closed behind him, he'd known he'd made a mistake. This was his place, one of the few places on the site where he could have a few moments to himself. But not anymore. He shared it with a memory from that morning, a memory of Pru ... and a kiss he couldn't forget.

Oh, he'd tried. There was always paperwork with a project the size of Fort Sam, and he had more than enough to keep him busy for hours. But in the echoing

silence that engulfed him, his concentration was shot to
hell. He couldn't hear himself think, couldn't hear
anything but the remembered roar of his blood in his
ears when he'd given in to the impossible needs that had
ripped through him the instant Pru had pressed her
mouth to his.

And in a moment of sheer insanity, he'd called her.

"No, I just..." Hell, what was he supposed to say?
I called you because I couldn't stop myself? Frus-
trated, he blurted, "Dammit, I don't know why I called.
I'm here at the office—"

"Oh, God, did something else happen?"

"No, and I'm going to make damn sure it doesn't.
I'm spending the night here until the bastard's caught."

Pru's breath lodged in her chest. "But couldn't that
be dangerous? What if he comes back?"

"I'll be ready for him," he said, the concern she
made no effort to hide turning his voice gruff. "What
are you doing?"

Caught off guard, Pru looked blankly around her
living room. What *had* she been doing, other than
thinking of him? "N-nothing much. Just watching
TV."

Silence stretched and grew, the kiss they'd shared
never mentioned but always there between them,
throbbing like a splinter under the skin, refusing to be
ignored. Her pulse jumping, Pru desperately searched
for something to say before he found an excuse to hang
up. But before she could think of anything, he was
breaking the silence for her. "So what are you watching?"

"Uh...the football game."

"You like football?"

She had to laugh at his surprise. "Are you kidding? With my family? When I was growing up, nothing short of a nuclear explosion could drag my dad and brothers away from the TV when a game was on. So you either learned to love it or you spent a lot of time by yourself."

"Yeah, my family was the same way."

"Really? I didn't know you had brothers and sisters."

"One of each," he said with a smile in his voice. "We drove my parents nuts competing with each other."

Pru laughed, fascinated by the image of a younger Zeb trying to one-up his siblings the way she had hers. "So did we. My mother was sure we were all going to turn out to be race car drivers."

He chuckled, and after that, it was easy. They talked about best friends and old relatives, favorite holidays and movies they could watch again and again. He teased her about the tearjerkers she loved to cry over, made her laugh, then forget time. When she finally glanced at the clock, she was shocked to discover it was going on eleven o'clock.

Still, she didn't want to hang up, didn't want to deny herself the husky murmur of his voice in her ear. But it was getting late and work at the site started early every morning. Reluctantly she said, "I hate to break this up, but it's getting late—"

"And you have to go to bed."

It was just a statement of fact, but something about the way he said it had her heart dropping to her stomach in a crazy rush. Suddenly the silence was back between them, this time fairly crackling with sexual tension. "Yes," she finally managed faintly. "I'm sorry—"

"Don't be. I've enjoyed it."

The husky admission wrapped around her like an unexpected hug, surprising her, warming her inside and out. "So have I," she said softly. "Good night." A slow smile playing around the corners of her mouth, she carefully replaced the receiver in its cradle. When she went to bed a short while later, she was still smiling.

The following day, she saw him at work, of course, her eyes meeting his across the width of the compound. All around them the crew was busy at work replacing the pipes damaged by the vandal, but they might have been alone for all the notice they paid the activity around them. Still, Pru managed to keep her distance, what conversation they had over the course of the day limited to business. But every time their eyes met, the silent messages that passed between them had nothing to do with work.

That night, Murdock called her again. Already in bed, trying to get through the latest bestselling murder mystery, Pru knew it was him the minute the phone rang. A happiness unlike anything she had known before dancing in her blood, she grinned as she recognized his voice, then settled down for a long talk that didn't once include the subject of work.

After that, the pattern of their days and nights was set. They spent the hours at the site watching each other from a distance, then the evenings on the phone. Like old friends who had known each other an eternity, they talked about anything and everything. And when they reluctantly hung up each night, knowing that it would only be a matter of hours before they saw each other again, the phone lines practically hummed with anticipation.

But on the third night, Zeb didn't call at his usual time. In fact, he didn't call at all. Restless, never one to sit patiently and wait for the phone, Pru prowled around her too quiet apartment, doubts tearing at her. Had he just been bored the past few nights and called her because he didn't have anything better to do? Maybe he'd found something—or *someone*—that interested him more and he didn't have any further need to talk to her.

Swearing, feeling like a teenager worrying about a boy for the first time in her life, she deliberately turned away from the maddeningly silent phone. But a few moments later she glared at it from across the room. Ring! she cried silently. Don't just lay there like a dead duck!

Call him.

The order came out of nowhere, a grim, resounding command in her head that seemed to come from her very soul. Startled, Pru never thought to question it. Snatching up the phone, she quickly dialed Zeb's office number at the site.

She didn't know how long she stood there next to her couch, the unanswered ringing of his phone echoing in her ears, before she became aware of the worry twisting in her stomach. Frowning, she tried to reason it away. There was probably a perfectly logical explanation why he wasn't answering. He could just be checking the site to make sure it was secure. Or he could have gone out with some of his friends. It was Wednesday night, and a lot of the crew liked to celebrate the middle of the week. Her teeth working her bottom lip, she hung up, warning herself not to be a fool.

Something's wrong.

As before, the heavy-toned voice came out of nowhere, echoing in her head like the voice of doom, refusing to be ignored. Startled, Pru paled, no longer questioning her own gut instinct or the guardian angel who seemed to be guiding her. Murdock was in trouble; she could feel it in her bones. Her heart hammering frantically, she rushed into her bedroom to change out of the nightshirt she'd pulled on earlier after her bath. Seconds later, her purse thrown over her shoulder and her car keys already in her hand, she hurried out her front door.

The rain that had started right after work slapped her in the face as she sprinted to her Jeep. Seconds later she was headed for Fort Sam, her eyes narrowed on the dark, slick road. Every instinct she possessed urged her to hurry, but it had rained nonstop for hours and in some low spots the water pooling on the pavement was deep and dangerous and impossible to judge in the dark. Her windshield wipers slapping ineffectually at the downpour, she struggled to keep her foot light on the accelerator.

The site, when she finally reached it, looked the same as usual. The security lights were on, but they barely made a dent in the thick shadows, and nothing moved but the rain dancing on the surface of the lakelike puddles that seemed to grow larger with every passing second. Braking to a quick stop, Pru looked wildly around and almost wilted when she saw Zeb's truck parked in its usual spot near the office. Wherever he had gone, he was back.

Almost giddy with relief, she chuckled suddenly at her paranoid imaginings. He would probably laugh at her for rushing over there like a nut just because he hadn't answered the phone, but she didn't care. Since she was here, she couldn't pass up the chance to see him again, especially when there was no one there but the two of them.

But when she gave a peremptory knock at the office door a few seconds later and quickly pushed it open, rain from the overhanging eaves dripping down the back of her neck, the office was empty. Between one heartbeat and the next, the worry that she had tried to shrug off as ridiculous was back.

She told herself not to panic, but it was too late. Her mouth was dry, her heart racing. Whirling from the office, she shouted hoarsely, "Zeb!" Her cry echoed unanswered in the wet darkness. A sob rising in her throat, she knew then that something was horribly wrong. If Zeb had just been out checking the site, he would have heard her and answered.

The rain beat down on her uncovered head and plastered her clothes to her body, but there was no time to go back to the Jeep for an umbrella. Fear nearly strangling her, she ran from the east wing to the main entrance, her eyes frantically searching, while deep inside a voice urged, *"Hurry. Hurry."*

She found him outside the west wing sprawled facedown and unmoving in a puddle.

"No!" She didn't remember moving, but suddenly she was throwing herself to the ground next to him and pulling his face out of the water. "Oh, God, please...please!"

Disjointed prayers spilling from her lips, she grabbed his shoulder to tug him over onto his back, tears spilling from her eyes when he coughed weakly, spitting up the water that surely would have drowned him if she hadn't come upon him when she had. But he was still unconscious. And so pale. The skin stretched taut against his chiseled cheeks was ashen, a stark contrast to his sodden, midnight black hair that was flattened to his forehead.

Unmindful of the water that pooled around her, she leaned over him to gently rest her palm against his whisker-roughened cheek. "Zeb? Can you hear me?"

Lying still as death, he didn't move so much as an eyelash. Then she saw the watery rivulet of blood that slowly seeped out from beneath the dark hair behind his left ear. Her heart stopped in midbeat.

"Oh, God!"

She had to get help... now! But how could she leave him this way? More scared than she'd ever been in her life, she lurched to her feet and carefully grabbed him under his arms. He outweighed her by a good thirty pounds or more, but it never entered her head that she couldn't move him. Grunting with the effort, she strained and tugged until she was finally able to move him. It was only inches, but it was enough so that his head and shoulders were out of the puddle and on higher ground.

Only then, when she knew there was no danger of him drowning, did she dare to leave him. "I'll be right back," she promised, praying he could hear her. "Just lie still and rest."

Drenched to the skin, she ran as if the hounds of hell were after her, sprinting to his office and the only phone on the site. Within seconds she'd called both an ambulance and the M.P.'s, and was turning to leave when she saw a double-size sleeping bag stretched out on the floor behind his desk. The only thing she'd seen she could cover him with, she snatched it up and ran back out into the rain.

He was right where she'd left him, his face turned up to the dark rain, his breathing slow and steady. Her heart squeezing at the sight of him, Pru felt her control slip and hastily blinked back the tears that mixed with rain in her eyes. She could fall apart later. Right now, he needed her.

Carefully spreading the sleeping bag over him, she dropped to her knees beside him. "Zeb? Can you hear me? It's Pru."

For a second she thought she saw his eyes flicker, but she couldn't be sure in the poor light. How long had he been out? Was he still bleeding? she wondered wildly. Afraid his life was slipping away while she just sat there, unable to do anything but twist her hands together, she reached over to carefully probe the wound behind his ear.

"Don't!"

The weak growl caught her off guard, startling her so that she jumped. Her heart thumping, her gaze flew to his, only to find him watching her with pain-clouded eyes. "Thank God!" she choked. "Don't move. I've called the M.P.'s and an ambulance is on the way."

Even as she spoke, the wail of a siren could be dimly heard in the rain. Now that someone else was rushing to handle the crisis, she could feel herself starting to come unraveled. Her eyes misted, and she leaned over him, the need to touch him more than she could bear. She traced the furrowed lines in his brow, her touch whisper soft. "How do you feel?"

"Like I've been run over by a truck," he said with a groan as he closed his eyes. "Give me a moment, and I'll be fine."

"And with the right clothes, I'm short and petite," she retorted. "Dammit, Zeb, you scared me to death!

Don't you dare think about getting up. The ambulance will be here any moment."

He opened one eye to give her an arched look. "Are you giving orders on my site, lady?"

"You're damn right," she retorted, drawing the sleeping bag snugger around his broad shoulders. "The man in charge is out of commission and I'm taking over. If you don't like it, tough. There's not a heck of a lot you can do about it. At least not right now."

"So you'd take advantage of a man when he's flat on his back in the mud," he teased weakly, the glint in his eyes promising retribution. "I hope you know that when I'm back on my feet, that's going to cost you."

He didn't know it, but nothing could have thrilled her more. Grinning, she took the hand he held out to her and linked her fingers with his. "I'm looking forward to it."

Seven

Pru followed the ambulance in her Jeep to the hospital, but by the time she found a parking place and hurried inside, Zeb had already been whisked away. The waiting room was packed, a result, the admitting nurse told her, of a string of traffic accidents brought on by the rainy weather. The doctors were working as fast as they could, but it would probably be a while before they got to Zeb, especially since he was conscious and didn't appear to be that seriously hurt. Resigned to a long wait, Pru had no choice but to find a seat.

She felt—and looked—like a drowned rat, but if anyone noticed her wet clothes and hair, they were polite enough not to stare. Puddles, however, were starting to form around her saturated Nikes, and she just couldn't sit there while a lake formed around her on the waiting room floor. Quickly telling the nurse she was going to wait outside under the protected entrance until she had dried a little, she started toward the automatic doors that led to the parking lot.

But she'd only taken two steps when the doors slid open suddenly and a man walked in with what appeared to be a television camera balanced on his shoulder. And right behind him was Gus Larson, a well-known but obnoxious investigative reporter for one of the local TV stations.

Surprised, Pru had a sudden, sinking feeling in her stomach. What was he doing here? Afraid to ask, she intended to walk right past him and his sidekick, but before she could step around the two men, the reporter moved to block her path. "You wouldn't happen to be Pru Sullivan, would you?"

Shocked that he knew her name, Pru glanced up, the feeling in her stomach turning lightning quick to dread. He knew. Somehow he'd found out what had happened at the site and his rat's nose could smell a story. She'd be damned if she'd help him uncover it.

Something in her face, however, must have tipped Larson off to the fact that he wasn't going to get anything but "no comments" out of her, because he was suddenly throwing questions at her. "I understand that Zebadiah Murdock was attacked at the building site of the new communications center at Fort Sam tonight and that you called for an ambulance. Aren't you a building inspector? What do you know about the vandalism at the site? And what's your connection with Murdock? What were you doing at the base at this time of night?"

Pru blanched. Behind her she felt the interested eyes of the people in the waiting room watching the unfolding scene with avid interest, but all she could think of was that her boss was going to be asking these and tougher questions if he ever heard about this.

The camera was running, the microphone Larson held pushed right in front of her mouth. Ignoring both, she asked, "How do *you* know about the vandalism, Mr. Larson? And who told you about the attack on Mr. Murdock?"

"I got an anonymous tip," he retorted. "So what's the scoop, Ms. Sullivan? What do you know about the problems Murdock has been having at the site?"

At the mention of an anonymous tip, Pru froze, hardly hearing the questions he threw at her. How could someone have known that she was at the site and had called for help unless they'd seen her? While she'd been frantically struggling to pull Murdock to higher ground, had someone been hiding in the darkness, watching, waiting for the chance to attack her, too?

Suddenly cold, desperately needing to see Zeb, she said stiffly, "I don't know anything. Now, if you'll excuse me, I have nothing more to say to you."

Pivoting, she whirled back toward the admitting desk and rushed through the double doors that led to the examining rooms. Alarmed, a nurse tried to stop her, but she was quicker and, as luck would have it, Zeb was in the first curtained cubicle.

"You just narrowly missed a concussion," a white-coated doctor was telling him as she slipped inside. "Go home and get a good night of uninterrupted sleep and you should feel a lot better in the morning."

Standing next to the examining table rebuttoning his damp shirt, Murdock spotted her, his eyes sharpening at the sight of her pale face. "Pru? What's wrong?"

"Gus Larson—"

"Miss, you can't come in here!" The nurse who had tried to block her way to the examining rooms swept back the curtain and scowled disapprovingly at Pru before glancing at the doctor. "I'm sorry, Doctor, I tried to stop her."

"Gus Larson is in the waiting room with a cameraman," Pru told Zeb quickly. "Somebody called him and told him about the attack and all the problems you've been having at the site and he's asking a lot of questions."

The doctor dismissed the nurse with the assurance that he would take care of the problem, then gave Murdock a wry look. "I'm not going to ask what this is about—I think I'd rather not know. The first hallway to the left will take you to a back entrance."

Murdock sighed in relief and held out his hand. "Thanks, Doctor. You don't know how I appreciate this."

Thanks to the doctor's help, they were able to slip out undetected and, within minutes, they'd left the hospital far behind. Taking a quick look in her rearview mirror to make sure Larson hadn't found a way to follow them, Pru glanced at Zeb, who sat in the passenger seat with his head back against the headrest and his eyes closed. Still pale, he looked tired.

"Where do you live?" she asked huskily.

It took a visible effort, but he was able to force his eyes open and sit up straighter. "Just take me back to the site. I'll be fine."

"No way, bud. You're going home to bed. Doctor's orders."

His eyes, dark with promise and amusement, met hers in the darkness. "Don't forget I'm keeping score," he warned softly. "You keep this up and I'm really going to look forward to collecting."

Her pulsing skipping, Pru struggled to hold back a smile. "I'm shaking in my shoes, Murdock. What's your address?"

He told her, simply because he didn't have the strength to deny her and, deep down inside, he had an inexplicable need to see her in his home. But the minute he unlocked his front door and escorted her into the carriage house, he watched her face light up with interest and knew he was in no shape to deal with her tonight. His head was pounding, he felt as weak as a kitten, and all he could think about was holding her.

"This is great!" she said excitedly, turning in a circle to observe the living room as a whole. Half the size of her entire apartment, it had ten-foot ceilings, wood floors and a carved oak fireplace mantel that was positively gorgeous.

"It still needs a lot of work."

"But it'll be worth it when you're finished." She would have liked to explore further, but she'd seen him rubbing his temples, and she knew his head had to be killing him. "Are you sure you're okay? Maybe you should have stayed the night at the hospital. You're awfully pale."

"I'll be fine," he assured her huskily. His shoulder propped against the doorjamb of the French doors that opened into the living room from the entrance hall, he didn't budge.

"You must have taken quite a hit." Concerned by the pain that still darkened his eyes, she started toward him. "You were out cold when I found you." Not able to think about how close he had come to drowning, she swallowed the sudden lump in her throat. "What happened?"

"I heard a noise and went to check it out. The next thing I knew, I was looking up at you."

A cold shiver raced up Pru's spine, chilling her to the bone. If she hadn't listened to that insistent voice in her head, if she hadn't come when she had, if the puddle he'd fallen into had been deeper, she never would have gotten to him in time. So many ifs, she thought, hugging herself. If her timing had been the slightest bit off, she would have lost him. Again.

Surprised by the odd thought, she frowned in growing puzzlement. How could she have lost him again when he'd never been hers to begin with?

"What's wrong?"

Lost in her thoughts, she blinked, shrugging off the odd thought. "Nothing. I was just thinking how I'd like to get my hands on the man who hit you. But we can talk about that tomorrow. The doctor said you needed to go right to bed, so if you'll show me where you keep your extra blankets, I'll just make myself comfortable right here on the couch—"

Still leaning against the doorjamb, Murdock straightened as if she'd pinched him. "Whoa, girl, back up a minute. Are you saying you're staying the night?"

"Well, of course," she said as if there'd never been any question of her doing anything else. "You shouldn't be alone."

Just the thought of her stretched out on his couch the rest of the night set his heart tripping over itself. "No!" He spoke more sharply than he'd intended, and at her look of surprise, he flushed. "I appreciate the thought, but you don't need to stay and baby-sit me. I'll be fine."

Not convinced, she eyed him suspiciously. "You're planning on going back to the site, aren't you?"

The thought had entered his head, but he wasn't stupid enough to tell her that. "No, of course not."

"Tell another one," she suggested, grinning. "That one didn't fly very well."

A chuckle rumbling through his chest, he wanted to shake her. The woman was downright dangerous when she got that sassy look in her eye, and he should insist that she leave now, while he could still let her go. But the words just wouldn't come.

Knowing he was making a mistake but unable to stop himself, he said roughly, "You don't need to do this, but if you're going to stay, you need to get out of those damp clothes."

Whatever Pru had been expecting, it wasn't that. Startled, her eyes wide, she stuttered, "O-oh, but th-that's n-not necessary—"

"What's the matter?" he teased. "Afraid I won't be able to control myself if I see you in my robe?"

"No, of course not—"

"Good. Because right now, honey, I haven't got the energy to spit. You're as safe as if you were in church. Go on in the bathroom and change. Down the hall, second room on the left. My robe's hanging on the back of the door."

He didn't wait to see if she followed his suggestion, but turned instead to the phone to call Lieutenant Barker. But the M.P. couldn't tell him much. No one saw his attacker and the bastard left no clues. Not surprised, Murdock thanked him, then replayed the messages on his answering machine. Only half listening, he was trying to figure out which one of his men was cold-blooded enough to leave him to die in the rain when a low, hoarse voice tore through his concentration. Stiffening, he stopped the tape and rewound it.

"You'd better listen and listen good, Murdock," an obviously disguised voice warned harshly. "That tap you got on the back of the head was just a warning. Quit the Fort Sam project or next time you won't be so lucky. And that favorite inspector of yours won't be around to save your ass, either. I'll make sure of it."

Snarling a fierce oath, Murdock stopped the tape, red-hot rage streaking through him at the thought of anyone threatening Pru. He could take care of himself, but she was an innocent in this, at the base only because she'd been assigned to the project by her boss. If the yellow-bellied coward on the tape valued his life, he'd damn well leave her alone or Murdock would make him regret the day he'd been born.

Reaching for the phone, he quickly called Barker back. "No, I didn't recognize the voice," he said after giving him a summary of the recorded threat. "It was disguised, but the bastard made his point. If I don't quit the project, he'll make sure Ms. Sullivan and I regret it."

Hearing a sudden gasp from the doorway, Murdock glanced up to find Pru standing at the entrance to the hall, and whatever he was going to say next to the lieutenant dried up and blew away. No woman had a right to look so sexy in a man's robe, he thought numbly as his eyes took a slow tour of her slender frame swallowed whole by the garment that only came to the middle of his calf but dragged the ground on her. Her hair was a mass of loose, wild chestnut curls on her shoulders, the forest green velour bringing out the deep, matching color of her eyes. God, she was beautiful!

And scared. Suddenly noticing how pale she was and the way her gaze kept skipping to the answering machine as if it was a rattler threatening to strike, he realized she'd heard enough of his side of the conversation to figure out that nothing about tonight had been an accident. Next time would be worse...for both of them.

Quickly promising the lieutenant he'd bring the tape in in the morning, he hung up. Silence, thick with questions, hung in the air as his eyes met hers. "So you heard."

Nerves knotting in her gut and her hands balled into fists in the pockets of his robe, Pru nodded. "Enough not to like the sound of it."

"You'd better sit down and hear the rest of it," he said flatly. Rewinding the tape, he played it again.

Seated on the couch, her bare feet curled under her, Pru hugged herself as the cold, hard words echoed off the living room's high ceilings. Fury. The caller's voice practically shook with barely controlled fury and a promise Pru couldn't help but take seriously. If Murdock didn't quit the Fort Sam project, he would pay a heavy price. And so would she.

"What are you going to do?" she asked when the tape ended and he turned off the machine with a jab of his finger.

"Not quit, that's for sure." His nerves strung too tight for him to relax, he prowled restlessly around the room. Trying not to notice how tempting she looked sitting on the couch in nothing but his robe, he deliberately avoided going within ten feet of where she sat. "Don't worry," he assured her. "I don't know who this bastard is, but he's not going to touch you."

"I'm not worried as much about me as I am about you," she confessed. "If he got to you once—"

"Until now, all the attacks were limited to the site. Next time I'll be ready." Frowning over something that had been nagging him, he turned toward her abruptly. "How did you know I was in trouble, anyway? You've never dropped by the site at night before. What were you doing there?"

She hadn't meant to tell him; she was sure he wouldn't want to know. But suddenly the words were spilling out and she could do nothing to stop them. "I was worried . . . I don't know why. But when you didn't call and I couldn't get you at the office, this crazy voice in my head kept telling me something was wrong."

"You heard a voice?"

At his skeptical look, Pru had to smile. "I know it sounds crazy, but I really do have both oars in the water. Somebody was trying to tell me something, and no matter how I tried to shrug it off, I just couldn't. Somehow, I *knew* you were in trouble. So I got dressed and came looking for you."

She was right—it did sound crazy. But even though he would have given anything to deny it, he knew exactly what she was talking about. He'd never considered himself a fanciful man, but ever since he'd met this woman, he'd felt a connection with her, a karmic link he'd never felt with anyone else in his life. It was almost as if there was a silent thread of communication between them, so that even when she was nowhere in sight, he was constantly aware of her presence in his life. And it was getting stronger with every passing day.

In no shape to deal with that now, he frowned. "When you got to the site, did you see anything?"

"No, nothing. After I found you, all I could think about was getting help. Since the jerk who hit you obviously knows I was there, he had to be hiding in the darkness watching the whole thing." Even now, when she knew she and Zeb were safe, the thought of someone watching them like a thief in the dark sent a shiver skating down her spine. "But with the rain and everything, I didn't see him."

"Neither did I," he muttered with a pained grimace, the throbbing in his head intensifying. "The bastard came up behind me and I never even got a look at him."

If she let him, he would spend the next hour discussing the attack, Pru thought as she pushed to her feet. But he looked ready to drop where he stood, and she should have insisted he go to bed the minute they'd walked in his front door. "Well, there's nothing we can do about it tonight. If you'll show me where those blankets are, you can get to bed before you fall on your face."

Tired, his head and neck one big ache, Murdock knew there was no arguing with her—the lady's chin had that "Don't mess with me, mister" set—but he couldn't in good conscience let her take the couch while he stretched out on the bed. "If you're going to stay, then take the bed."

"Watch it, bud," she warned, her eyes dancing. "You've already got one knot on your head. You don't want another one. Now, will you go to bed? *Please.*"

He needed to—while he still had the energy to make it to his bedroom. But after he found her some blankets and a pillow, he stood at the entrance to the living room, unable to take his eyes from her as she curled up on his couch as if she intended to stay as long as necessary. He could, he realized, get used to having her there, in his home, within reach.

His heart started to hammer in time with the sharp cadence striking a raw nerve behind his eyes, and he turned away. Because he had to. Because if he didn't, he was going to do something incredibly stupid and no doubt make a fool of himself at one and the same time. Because he couldn't handle what the lady did to him . . . not now, maybe not ever.

Considering the way his head was pounding and every nerve in his body was tight with need for the woman spending the night on his couch, he never expected to fall asleep. Instead he slept like the dead. He'd been positive she wouldn't be able to move without him being aware of it, so conscious was he of her presence in his home, but in actuality, he didn't know a thing after his head hit the pillow. Exhaustion rushed up to embrace him, and he was out for the count.

Bone-weary, he should have slept like a baby through the night. But sometime after midnight, when the neighborhood was at its quietest and even the most dedicated night owls had retreated to their beds, the indignant, hostile barking of a dog two houses down was like the cry of an alarm in the night. His head half buried under his pillow, Murdock came abruptly, rudely awake.

For all of thirty seconds he just lay there, trying to figure out why the back of his head was throbbing like the devil. Then memory came rushing back and, with a muttered curse, he threw off the bedclothes and rolled to his feet, instantly alert as the barking of the dog registered. If the bastard who'd hit him had decided to follow him home to finish the job, he was in for a hell of a surprise. He was ready for him.

But as he moved to the window that overlooked his neighbor's house, someone yelled, the dog quieted, and a huge rat silently glided away on a power line. Just making the rodent out in the blackness of the night, Murdock chuckled. So much for bogeymen sneaking around in the dark.

Relieved, he padded into the kitchen to make sure the back door was securely locked, then checked each window as he soundlessly made his way in the dark through the rest of the lower floor. Outside, the neighborhood was once again as quiet as a tomb.

He really did intend to go back to bed. But as he started to pass the French doors that opened from the entrance hall into the living room, Pru's shadowy figure asleep on the couch drew his gaze like a magnet.

She lay on her side, clutching the pillow he'd given her earlier to her chest, the blankets that should have been covering her dragging on the floor. The night was a cool one, though, and the thick robe she wore didn't offer nearly enough warmth. Curled into a ball, her bare feet tucked under the robe's hem, she looked cold and uncomfortable.

A man with even a shot glass full of self-preservation would have known not to go anywhere near the lady right then. She'd wake up when she got cold enough and find the cover herself. But even as he sternly ordered himself not to be an idiot, he started toward her. His bare feet not making a sound on the wood floor, he reached down for the cover and carefully draped it over her.

The dream was so real, Pru could have reached out and touched it. Zeb . . . holding her as if he would never let her go, loving her, assuring her in a voice that seemed to echo in her soul that she was his and always had been. Smiling, murmuring his name, she felt warmth envelope her and opened sleepy eyes to find him leaning over her, his hands curled into the quilt he was in the process of gently pulling up to her shoulders. Caught in the folds of her dreams, she reached for him.

"Pru . . . honey . . ."

If all cylinders had been up and running, she would have heard the reluctant protest in his voice as he hesitated against the pull of her arms sliding around his neck. But he was finally there, during the darkest part of the night, when she'd ached for him for years without even knowing his name. Joy flooding her, she pulled him down to her, her mouth finding his in the darkness.

Madness tugging at him, Murdock groaned at the feel of her against him. He shouldn't be here, shouldn't let her pull him down to the couch with her, shouldn't let her kiss him. She wasn't fully awake, for God's sake, and only a jerk would take advantage of a woman when she didn't know what she was doing.

But, Lord, she moved and kissed and seduced like a woman who knew exactly what she was doing. He couldn't think, couldn't breathe without drawing in the scent of her rain-washed body. And the feel of her under him—God, it was enough to drive a normally rational man right out of his head.

Wanting, needing to touch every sweet inch of her, his hands fumbled for the belt of his robe where it was tied at her impossibly small waist. Just this once, he promised himself as her mouth nibbled at his, her tongue teasing and wooing and damnably clever. His blood starting to pound in his veins, his mind clouding, he struggled to concentrate on the task at hand, cursing the stubborn knot until it abruptly gave.

With a grunt of satisfaction, he lifted both hands to the lapels and parted them with fingers, he noted to his amazement, that were suddenly trembling. Taken aback, he tried to remember the last time any woman had shaken him so badly, but the only one he could think of was the one in his arms. Unconsciously holding his breath, he unwrapped the robe.

Perfect. Even bathed in shadows, with her green eyes dark pools of mystery, and the only light the glow of the streetlight half a block away, he could see she was gorgeous. Legs that were long and tempting flared into sensuous hips and full breasts that were made for a man's hands—*his* hands. It made no sense, but he knew as clearly as if he'd touched her a thousand times that she was his. Had always been his...down through time immemorial.

Stunned, he shook his head, trying to clear it. *How the hell could he know that? He needed to think....*

But all he could think of was her. The silky cream that was her skin. The wild mane of her chestnut hair. The feel of her slim hips in his hands. How her pouting nipples would taste in his mouth. How she confused and delighted and seduced him just by smiling into his eyes. Groaning, he kissed her as if there was no yesterday or tomorrow, only now, this moment that couldn't last.

Her hands climbing his back, her mouth hot and hungry under his, Pru never thought to question what had brought him from his bed to hers. Slowly, lingeringly, her hands trailed over him, reacquainting themselves with the powerful lines of a man who should have been a stranger but wasn't. She'd waited so long, she thought deep in her soul, her fingers sliding over his back and shoulders and down to the boxer shorts that covered his hips. It seemed like she'd been waiting forever....

He moaned, every muscle in his body seeming to tighten with need. Without questioning the how or why of it, she knew right where to touch him to draw a groan from him, just how to tease him to drive him wild. Murmuring his name, wanting him so badly she positively ached, she slipped her fingers under his shorts.

He made a rough sound in his throat and moved lightning quick, shedding his shorts and pulling his robe from her. When he came back down to her, the quilt pulled up to his shoulders, covering them, it was just the two of them, naked, bare and hot. In the darkness, his eyes glowed down at her. "Now touch me, honey. I've dreamed of having your hands on me."

He hadn't meant to make that admission, but then her hand closed around him and he couldn't think at all. She stroked an urgency in him, a heat that burned like liquid fire. He'd always thought himself a considerate lover, a man who knew how to hang on to his control until his partner was satisfied. But with one touch, he knew he'd finally found the one woman who could test his control.

A growl of raw need rumbling up from his chest, he moved over her like a hot desert wind, heating her inside and out with his mouth and hands and lean, hard body. With sure, knowing fingers, he charted every inch of her, caressing, kissing, nuzzling her until her blood was rushing through her veins, her pulse throbbing, her bones melting. Shuddering, her cries of surprise echoing in the darkness, she clutched at him as if even now she was afraid that she would lose him, her sea green eyes dazed and dark with desire.

And something in the total innocence of her response clicked in his passion-fogged brain. He stilled, his heart slamming against his ribs, his hand gentle as it cupped her cheek. "Have you done this before, sweetheart?"

In love for the first time in her life, she never thought to lie. Turning to press a kiss into his palm, she smiled. "I've been waiting for you."

The admission terrified him. And moved him as nothing ever had or would again. An emotion he couldn't put a name to welling hot and thick in his throat, he kissed her softly, tenderly, his arms slipping around her to gather her close to his wildly beating heart. "Then we'll take it nice and slow," he whispered huskily. "Just relax. I'll take care of everything."

He left her for a moment only to get the protection that he kept in a nightstand drawer next to his bed, then he was back, taking her into his arms, warming her, murmuring to her in the dark. Just as he'd promised, his kisses were slow and drugging, his hands leisurely, thorough. With every touch, every kiss, every rub of his naked body against hers, he caressed and fondled and seduced, drawing out the pleasure until she was mindless. And even when she moved under him, with him, her hips lifting blindly to his, he somehow found the control he needed.

But it couldn't last. He wanted her too much, needed her more than his next breath, ached for her until he burned. And the lady's patience was as sorely tested as his. Whispering her need for him, she closed her fingers around him and gently guided him to the wet, hot heart of her desire.

Slowly, carefully, he eased into her, murmuring reassurances, the need to rush overwhelmed by a tenderness that clutched at his heart. Afraid he'd hurt her, he waited for a heartbeat, holding his breath. Then she smiled at him, lifted her hips and took him impossibly deeper. Just that quickly, he was lost.

Eight

————

Caught up in the magic of the night, he couldn't bring himself to let her go even when common sense tried to tell him it was the wise thing to do. So he swept her up into his arms and carried her off to his bed, where he'd dreamed of having her from the moment he'd first laid eyes on her. Just needing to hold her, he wrapped her close, her back snug against his and her thighs molding his. He pulled the covers over them and closed his eyes with a sigh, more content than he could ever remember being in his life. Within seconds, they were both asleep.

With the rising of the sun the next morning, however, reality returned with a vengeance.

Lying on his back, he came awake abruptly to find Pru draped over him, her face buried against his shoulder as if he was her favorite pillow, her bent leg thrown over his thigh beneath the covers. His pulse accelerating to warp speed, he froze, memories of the night hitting him like an avalanche, stealing his breath. Dear God, what had he done?

She'd been a virgin, an innocent. The minute she'd told him, he should have gotten the hell away from her. Dammit, how could he have let this happen? He'd known he was light-years too old for her in both experience and age. But she'd looked up at him with her heart in her eyes, confessed that she'd been waiting for him, and none of that had seemed to matter. The old house could have come tumbling down around them, and he still wouldn't have found the strength to leave her.

So he'd stayed . . . when he should have run like hell. Because he hadn't just made love to her. He'd turned himself inside out for her in a way he had for no other woman. In a way he'd never *wanted* to for any woman.

She could break his heart.

The thought hit him like a pitcher of ice water, shocking him. No! She was barely more than a kid with stars in her eyes, caught up in an unreasonable attraction that couldn't last. He knew that, dammit, and there was no way he was letting the lady get to him! He would talk to her, make her see that he wasn't the young Prince Charming she should be holding out for—but not in bed. Carefully untangling himself from her arms, he eased out from under the covers and soundlessly made his way to the bathroom.

Pru woke minutes later to find herself in Zeb's bed without really remembering how she'd gotten there. Nothing, however, could erase the memory of his loving. It was the most incredible thing that had ever happened to her. How could she have known that making love, *falling* in love, could be so heart-stoppingly wonderful? Feeling like she could hug the whole world, she stretched luxuriously. It was only then that she saw Zeb standing in the doorway.

A slow smile started to slide across her mouth. "Good morning," she began huskily, only then noticing he wasn't nearly as happy as she was this morning. In fact, his expression was positively grim. Her mouth suddenly dry and her smile fading fast, she swallowed. She might not have any experience with mornings after, but she knew regret when she saw it in a man's eyes.

When he only returned her greeting with a stiff nod, she scooted to a sitting position and pulled the sheet to her neck, feeling awkwardly naked as she saw he was already dressed for the site in jeans, blue work shirt and boots. "I guess I don't have to ask if last night was as wonderful for you as it was for me," she said, breaking the tense silence. "Obviously it wasn't."

A dead man couldn't have ignored the pain in her eyes and voice, and he was far from dead where she was concerned. Wanting to cross to her, wishing he could hold her, and knowing it was impossible, he stayed where he was. "I don't want to hurt you, honey, but last night was a mistake that can't happen again."

"Why? Are you going to stand there and say it didn't mean anything to you? That you didn't feel the magic?"

Oh, he'd felt it, all right. And so had Grandpa when he'd hit his forties. "What I'm saying," he said tightly, "is that there's no future in this. There can't be—there are too many years between us. Somewhere out there, there's a man for you, someone who's young and just as eager to get started with his life as you are, someone who's not old enough to be your father."

Pain squeezing her heart, Pru could only stare at him. After the night they'd just shared, he couldn't possibly expect her to walk away as if it never happened. "But I don't want some other man!" she cried. "I never have. Don't you understand? You're the only one I've ever wanted!"

"Don't *do* that!"

His exasperated roar startled them both. Confused, she frowned. "Don't do what?"

"Talk as if I'm the one you've been waiting for all your life," he said, scowling. "A couple of weeks ago you didn't even know my name."

She could hear the panic in his voice, see the denial in the rigid set of his shoulders, and suddenly his anger made sense. He was afraid! Her smile soft and loving, she shrugged. "Maybe not, but deep inside I think I've always known you would come along for me to lo—"

"Stop right there," he growled before she could use the L word. "You're not thinking clearly right now, so you can't possibly know how you feel. Once you have some time to yourself, you'll feel differently."

"No, I won't," she argued, desperately looking around for something to wear. "I'm not some teeny-bopper with her head in the clouds who falls in and out of love every time the weather changes. I know how I feel. I love you—"

"No, you don't!"

"Yes, I do. And that isn't going to change tomorrow or next month or when we're both old and gray. If that bothers you, I'm sorry, but there's nothing I can do about it. Dammit, where are my clothes?"

Crossing to his closet, he pulled a shirt from a hanger and tossed it to her. "Has it crossed your mind that when you're old and gray I'll probably be six feet under?" he retorted caustically. And with nothing more than that, he stormed out, ordering over his shoulder,

"Get dressed. I don't know about you, but I've got to get to work."

Hurt, furious, frustrated, Pru threw a pillow after him. But just as her declaration of love had failed to reach him, the fluffy missile fell harmlessly to the floor.

The drive to work was a lesson in torture. Since Zeb's truck was still at the site and Pru had only the stiff and dirty clothes she'd worn the night before, Zeb had to ride with her to her apartment so she could change, then sat like a statue in the passenger seat while she drove to the site. The minute they arrived, he curtly thanked her for the ride and stalked off.

Her heart one big bruise in her chest, Pru caught only glimpses of him for the next three hours. She knew he was avoiding her and she tried to give him the space he needed. But it wasn't easy. From the grumbling of some of the men, it soon became obvious that Murdock was quietly questioning them, trying to feel them out about their whereabouts at the time he was attacked the night before. Since the M.P.'s had already asked the same questions, the crew was feeling the pressure and most of them didn't care for the cloud of suspicion hanging over their heads.

She wanted to go to him then, be by his side, offer him silent support for what was proving to be a difficult situation. But every time their eyes chanced to meet, she saw denial flash in the dark blue depths and she stayed where she was. She couldn't, however, make any promises for how long she could continue because every instinct she possessed was crying out for her to grab the big lug by those impossibly broad shoulders and lay a kiss on him that would curl his hair. Right there in front of the entire crew and God Himself.

Maybe then, he'd finally admit that he was just as crazy about her as she was about him.

"Hey, Pru!" Roy Wilkins shouted at her from the office doorway, distracting her from her musings. "There's a call for you. It's your boss."

She paled, sudden dread dropping into her stomach as she made her way across the compound. Even before she stepped into the office and picked up the phone lying on Zeb's desk, she knew what was coming. "Good morning, Mr. James," she greeted him with a forced cheerfulness. "How are things at the office this morning?"

"Don't try to charm me, Ms. Sullivan," he warned coldly. "I got a call from Gus Larson a few minutes ago, and you've got some explaining to do. Like, why there are some major problems at the Fort Sam site and I'm just now hearing about them."

Pru winced as his voice rose toward a roar with each succeeding word. "I can explain—"

"You're damn right you'll explain. Get over here. *Now!*" He slammed down the phone without giving her a chance to so much as sputter a protest.

"Trouble?" Roy asked as she hung up.

She nodded, the rueful smile she managed to drag on not quite reaching her eyes. "With a capital *T.* I've got to put in an appearance at the office. One of those command performance things," she said, wrinkling her nose in a grimace. "I'm not sure when I'll be back."

Braced for the worst, she walked into Bruce James' office fifteen minutes later and greeted him with a cool nod. She'd hoped to keep this civilized, but she saw in an instant that that wasn't going to be possible. Not even offering her a seat, he leaned back in his chair and scowled at her like a principal calling a third-grader on the carpet for chewing gum in the library.

But she was no longer a child, and it took more than a hard glare from James's beady eyes to intimidate her. Not waiting for an invitation, she sank into one of the chairs in front of his desk, her back ramrod straight. "As I told you on the phone, I can explain about the problems at the base."

"Then you'd better start talking because you led me to believe everything was fine at the site when you knew damn well it wasn't. Unless you can come up with a damn good reason for lying to me, I've got all the grounds I need to fire you."

He was deliberately taunting her and enjoying every minute of it. Grinding her teeth, it was all Pru could do not to snap back at him. But she wasn't independently wealthy and government jobs weren't all that easy to find. "I didn't lie," she said stiffly. "As far as my duties at the site, everything has gone fine. The core samples on the cement were close to borderline, but they passed, and all the other work has passed inspection. End of story."

"Oh, really? And what about the matter of a little cement in the open pipes? And the use of imports? This is a government project, Sullivan. I shouldn't have to tell you that means mainly made in the U.S.A."

"Those were Murdock's problems, not mine. Everything was fixed after the vandalism, and the imports were a mix-up. American-made materials were bought, so I have no complaints. Everything has been aboveboard and professional."

"Except your relationship with Murdock," he said silkily, satisfaction curling his mouth as he pounced like a cat on a helpless canary. "You've been seeing him, haven't you?"

"No," she began, but even to her own ears, the denial sounded pitifully weak. Cursing the heat climbing in her cheeks, she tried again. "We have a good working relationship. That's all it is. If you don't believe me, ask Murdock. He'll tell you the same thing."

"I don't need to ask him. You were at the site last night when you had no business being there. And don't try to tell me you were working overtime. The only thing you were inspecting at that hour of the night was Murdock."

He made it sound dirty and sleazy, and Pru wanted to punch him in the mouth for it. Her green eyes hostile, she stood, no longer prepared to treat the little worm with any degree of civility, even if it did mean losing her job. "Since you've obviously already made up your mind about this, I can't see any reason to continue this discussion. If you're going to fire me, go ahead and do it and get it over with."

He wanted to, she could see it in his eyes. He was just dying to get rid of her, but he only shook his head. "And have you go to the Equal Employment Opportunity office because I haven't got any real proof that your relationship with Murdock is actually a conflict of interest? I don't think so."

The relief that hit Pru almost weakened her knees. But it was short-lived. Seeing her drag in a steadying breath, James smiled nastily. "Don't start celebrating just yet. I'm yanking you off the Fort Sam project. Head out to Lackland after lunch. Tom Rector's out sick today and you can sub for him the rest of the day. Tomorrow, the two of you are switching assignments.

Now get out of here. I've got work to do and so do you."

Long after Murdock saw Pru leave the site, he told himself it was none of his business where she went during the middle of the day. If she wanted to take some time off, it was no skin off his back. When she didn't come back at all later that afternoon, he told himself he wasn't concerned. He wasn't her boss and she didn't answer to him.

Forcing her from his thoughts, he spent what was left of the day arranging for a security guard to stay at the site at night. He should have sprung for a professional from the moment he realized there was a problem, but by then his budget was already tight and he hadn't wanted to put himself any more in the hole than he already was. But after last night, he no longer had a choice.

Whoever hit him wouldn't get a second chance.

But when he went home that night and faced the couch where he'd made love to Pru, she was there in his thoughts as clearly as if she stood in front of him. And there was no getting rid of her. Even though he kept his hands busy stripping the kitchen cabinets of decades of paint, his mind was free to wander, and she was all he could think of. The flash of her dimples. The feel of her arms drawing her down to him. The liquid heat of her closing around him.

He almost broke down and called her then, just as he had the nights he'd spent at the site. But he couldn't forget the look in her eyes when she'd told him she loved him. She'd meant every word. And that scared the hell out of him, because he wanted to believe her. In spite of the fact that she was hardly more than a kid. In spite of

the fact that she was obviously thinking with her heart
instead of her head. In spite of everything.

His expression stony, he returned his attention to the
cabinets, flatly refusing to even glance at the phone.
Deep down inside, however, he half expected her to call
him. If she called the site and got the security guard, she
would realize that he was at home. Since his number
was in the book, all she had to do was look it up.

She didn't.

By the time he went to bed hours later, he had no
choice but to conclude that she must have come to her
senses, just as he had predicted she would. He should
have been relieved. Instead he felt like breaking something.

The next morning he was in a bear of a mood. The
wound behind his ear was healing nicely, but he hadn't
slept well. When he hadn't been dreaming of Pru, he'd
lain awake in the dark trying to figure out which member of his crew was vicious enough to not only conspire
with his competitors, but also knock him over the head
and leave him for dead. He hadn't come up with a single name.

On top of all that, there was still Pru to deal with.
Was she going to be able to work with him now that
she'd apparently let go of the crazy idea that she was in
love with him? He'd been damn hard on her, and he
wouldn't blame her if she cut him dead the minute she
saw him.

But an hour after he arrived at work, when he still
hadn't caught sight of Pru anywhere, he started to
worry. Where the hell was she? It didn't take him long
to find out. He was in the east wing, arguing with one
of the tile layers over the installation of the ceramic
floor, when a tall, redheaded bean pole of a stranger

approached him and held out his hand. "Nice to meet you, Murdock. I heard you've been having a few problems with vandals. I'm Tom Rector. The new inspector."

Already in the act of accepting the other man's handshake, Murdock stiffened, his blue eyes instantly razor sharp. "New inspector? What happened to Ms. Sullivan?"

"We switched places. She's taking over the Lackland job."

So she wasn't coming back. The knowledge ripped through him like a rusty knife, the strength of the pain surprising him even as he tried to assure himself it was for the best. Aside from their personal relationship, she was safer working another job. He hadn't forgotten the threat left on his answering machine, the warning that had also included Pru. Until he could get his hands on the sleaze, he would sleep better knowing she was miles away and out of harm's way.

"Did she ask to be reassigned?" he asked stiffly, then wanted to kick himself for caring one way or the other. Why the hell did it matter? He'd gotten through to her—wasn't that what he'd wanted?

Tom shrugged. "Dunno. You'll have to ask her or call the boss and get the scoop from him. All I know is I got a call to report here today. Now, what can you tell me about these vandals? I'd like to know what we're dealing with."

"So would I," Murdock replied, and proceeded to tell him everything he could about the present situation.

But as he rattled on about the crises that had plagued the site for months now, it was Pru who dominated his thoughts. Was she okay? Had he hurt her so badly that she couldn't even stand to look him in the face again? And if that was what he wanted, why did he feel so sick inside? What the hell had he done?

That worry nagged at him all day, making it impossible for him to concentrate. Lieutenant Barker had picked up the tape from his answering machine, then reported back to him that afternoon that the M.P.'s had been able to discover little about the man who had almost killed him. Whoever he was, the bastard had been careful to time the attack between the scheduled rounds the M.P.'s made past the building site. On a rainy night when most people had been holed up inside, it wasn't surprising that no one had seen anything. With threats now being made at his home, it was also no longer just a base problem. Barker was now working with the San Antonio police, but they had nothing to go on but the tape, and the investigation had more or less ground to a halt.

He should have spent the rest of the day narrowing down the list of suspects. He didn't like distrusting any of his crew, but as far as he knew, none of them was in line for sainthood. Not that most of them weren't good, honest men. But money was a powerful temptation, especially when you didn't have any of your own. When your finances were desperate and someone was holding out cash, it was easy to rationalize away the scruples of a lifetime. All he had to do was figure out which one of his men was not only trying to lose this job for him, but also kill him.

But instead of focusing on who his enemies were, he found himself searching the site for Pru, wanting to talk to her. He missed her, dammit, and the knowledge shook him. When had she carved a notch for herself in his heart?

Cursing her, wanting her, he couldn't get away from the site fast enough at the end of the day. But things were no better at home. He took one look at the naked kitchen cabinets and all he could think of was the hours he'd spent on them last night, thinking of Pru. Determined not to make that same mistake tonight, he grabbed his basketball from the hall closet and headed out the back door to the basketball hoop he'd attached to the garage the first week he'd moved in. He'd shoot hoops until he was too tired to think. Maybe then he'd be able to get the lady out of his head.

An hour later he was drenched in sweat and bone-tired—not from the exercise but from fighting the inevitable. Swearing, he went inside for a hot shower that did nothing to ease his foul mood. The lady had put a spell on him, he decided irritably as he toweled off. And it was high time he did something about it.

Pru was picking at a tasteless frozen dinner when the doorbell rang, shattering the oppressive silence that hung heavy in the air of her apartment. Her eyes flying to the front door, she couldn't stop the sudden hope that rushed through her veins. But even as her heart told her it was Zeb, her head mockingly scoffed at the notion. The man wanted nothing to do with her; he'd made that brutally clear. And the sooner she accepted that, the sooner she could start forgetting him and stop crying over him every time the wind whispered his name in her ear.

Blinking the moisture from her eyes, she ignored another peal of the bell. She was in no mood for visitors, no mood to talk to anyone. The past two days had been the worst of her life. No man had ever broken her heart before—she didn't know how to deal with it, how to handle the pain. Then, on top of that, she had had to report to a new assignment when all she'd wanted to do was crawl into her bed and stay there until the hurting stopped.

Without warning, a thundering knock suddenly rattled the door, startling a gasp from her. "Pru? Are you in there? Dammit, woman, open the door!"

Later, Pru swore her heart stopped in midbeat. Zeb! He was here, he'd come just when she was beginning to despair of ever seeing him again. Tears welling in her throat, she surged to her feet and rushed to the door, her smile bright with joy.

But when she fumbled with the dead bolt and finally pulled the door open, the man who stood on her doorstep was anything but happy to see her. Dressed in black slacks and a blue and red shirt, his jaw clean-shaven and his hair still damp from a recent shower, he scowled down at her with dark, angry eyes.

"I'm all wrong for you," he said harshly.

It wasn't the greeting she'd dreamed of. In fact his tone was downright resentful. But he was there and talking and that was more than she'd hoped for last night. Miserably lonely, she'd waited for him to call, sure he would want to find out what had happened to her when she'd left the site and didn't return. But the phone hadn't rung, and she hadn't been able to bring herself to call him, instead. Every time she'd thought of swallowing her pride, she could hear him telling her that making love with her had been nothing but a mistake.

And now he was here to repeat the message just in case she hadn't gotten it. Suddenly it was too much. Her green eyes shooting daggers at him, she snapped, "So you said yesterday. If that's all you came for—"

She started to shut the door in his face, but he was too quick for her. His hand flew up to catch the door, and when it came to a power struggle, there was never any question of who was going to win. Sudden amusement glinting in his eyes as she tried to pull the door from his grasp and slam it shut, his mouth curled into a mocking grin. "What I came for is to prove a point. We're going out. You want to change or go as you are?"

"Out? But—"

He ran his eyes over her, noting the way the jeans and green sweater she wore hugged her slender figure. "Maybe you'd better put on something else," he said hoarsely. "Don't worry, we're not going anywhere fancy, but you'd probably feel more comfortable in something besides jeans."

Pru meant to argue, to flatly refuse to go anywhere with him, but the heat of his gaze dried up the air in her lungs. Without quite realizing how it happened, she found herself whispering faintly, "I'm fine just the way I am."

"Suit yourself," he said with a shrug. "Let's go."

She should have at least asked where he was taking her, but she suddenly didn't care. She was with him again, within touching distance when he bundled her into his truck, and nothing else seemed to matter. She could have sat like that for hours, content just to have him near.

It wasn't until he pulled into the parking lot of a popular nightclub that she remembered his promise to prove to her once and for all that he was all wrong for her. Eyeing the place suspiciously, she asked, "What are we doing here?"

"Come inside and I'll show you," he replied, and pushed open his door.

It was called the Time Warp and was one of the hottest gathering places in town for baby boomers. Pru had never been there herself, but as she stepped inside, it was easy to see why it was so popular. The lighting was subtle, the dance floor crowded and intimate, the music limited to anything and everything from the fifties and sixties. Even on a Thursday night, the place was packed, and Pru could see why. The music was hot, with the kind of beat that made it impossible to stand still. She loved it.

Her foot starting to tap, she glanced up at Murdock the minute he followed her inside, her smile bright and expectant. "*This* is what you wanted to show me?"

Her reaction not quite what he'd expected, he frowned at the sparkle in her eyes. "You like it here?"

"Of course!" she replied, clearly surprised that he might have thought differently. "The music's great. Who's that singing?"

"The Classic Four," he said, the flash of his eyes triumphant, guiding her out of the flow of traffic near the front door. "Which just proves the point I was trying to make. There's just too many years between us, honey. We have nothing in common."

"That's not true!"

"Of course it is. I grew up listening to the Beach Boys and the First Edition, not to mention who knows how many other bands that were two-hit wonders you've never heard of. I lost friends in Vietnam before you were even born—"

Her eyes flashed at that. "So I couldn't possibly understand what that time was like, right? That's bull, and you know it, Murdock. I've been to the Wall in D.C. I've seen the names of the men who died, the sheer waste. If you think I could see that and not be moved, then you don't know me at all.''

She was right. He knew exactly how the Wall must have shaken her, how she would have tried to brush the tears away before anyone saw. Muttering a curse, he tried one more time to reach her. ''Dammit, will you at least listen to the point I'm trying to make? By the time you started first grade, I was already starting my business.''

''Then I've got some catching up to do,'' she retorted, smiling teasingly. ''But not as much as you think.'' The music shifted then, turning slow and romantic. Her eyes sparkling, she held out her hand. ''Now that we've got that settled, how about a dance? This song's too good to miss.''

Scowling at her, he knew he shouldn't touch her. In fact, if he had any sense, he'd hustle her out to his truck and take her home before she made him forget that this was *not* a date. But he could feel himself weakening, the need to hold her twisting his heart in knots. And the song was a good one.

Her pulse starting to skip, Pru knew the minute he stopped fighting and gave in. The tense set of his jaw eased and his eyes warmed as they locked with hers. Laughing, her heart singing, she grabbed his hand and pulled him with her out onto the dance floor.

The song was one of her favorites, one she'd known for as long as she could remember. As Zeb's arms closed around her and anchored her against his heart, she felt as if she were dancing on air. A stern voice warned her that nothing had changed—he was stubbornly determined to throw roadblocks between them—but she hadn't been this close to him since they'd made love, and she refused to be discouraged. Slipping her hand at his shoulder behind his neck, she melted against him and started to hum. But she was too happy to hold back the emotions bubbling up in her and within seconds she was softly singing the words against his chest.

Surprised, Murdock stopped in his tracks. "You know the words to this?"

Smiling, she snuggled closer. "Mmm-hmm." Seeing his puzzlement, she couldn't hold back a grin. "Did I forget to mention that I'm the baby of the family and my oldest brother is only a couple of years younger than you? I grew up listening to this stuff."

Nine

His gaze narrowed on the too innocent glint in her green eyes, Murdock struggled with the sudden maddening urge to kiss that flirtatious grin off her mouth. How was he supposed to make her admit he was too old for her when the whole reason he'd brought her here had suddenly backfired in his face? Little witch. What was he going to do with her?

In answer, his body tightened in response, images of the one night they'd had together flashing in his head like a siren's smile, tempting the hell out of him. With a will of their own, his arms wrapped her close, until her breasts and hips brushed against him with the subtle, seductive movements of the dance. Heat spiraled through him, setting off fire alarms in his head, but still he couldn't bring himself to release her.

"So this music was part of your childhood," he drawled. "I don't suppose it would do any good to point out that I was already an adult by the time you heard it for the first time, would it?''

"Not a bit." She chuckled. ''I don't care if you were a hundred and one. I've got you right where I want you and I'm not letting you go.''

If he'd found it hard keeping his head until then, it was impossible after that. It seemed as if he'd been fighting the pull she had on his senses forever, but he just couldn't do it anymore, not when she was this close, this trusting in his arms. Not when she was right where his heart told him she belonged.

They danced for what seemed like hours, taking every opportunity to softly, gently rub against each other and slowly, oh, so slowly drive each other out of their minds. The cadence of the music may have changed, but it could have turned into a rumba for all the attention they paid it. Their steps lazy and seductive, they swayed to a rhythm that was uniquely their own, the heat in their eyes hot enough to start a blaze that could have burned the whole place down.

It was slow torture, the kind that could bring a man to his knees. Every nerve in his body screaming for more than just the tempting brush of thigh against thigh, Murdock felt his control balance on a sharp edge and knew he had to get out of there before he made a complete fool of himself.

"Come on," he said roughly. Grabbing her hand, he pulled her after him through the crowd like a man with the devil on his tail.

Hurrying to keep up with his long strides, Pru gasped as he dragged her outside into the cool night air. "Zeb, slow down! What's wrong?''

He turned on her so fast, she didn't have time to do anything but blink before she found herself pressed up against the nearest car and Zeb's mouth hot and hard on hers. Without a thought to their surroundings or who might step outside and chance upon them, she moaned and wound her arms around his neck.

He'd only meant to give her a quick kiss, something to hold him over until he could get her alone and naked in a warm, dark place where there wasn't another living soul within shouting distance. But the minute he touched her and she melted against him, and her mouth opened sweetly, hungrily under his, his brain fogged. A groan rippling through him, he tasted her, seduced her, his tongue dancing with hers in the wet, hot heat of her mouth.

The metal of the car cold against her back and hips, the night air chilly as it whispered over her hot skin, Pru felt nothing but Zeb pressed against her, heard nothing but the roar of her blood in her ears. Turning to putty in his arms, she clung to him as if she'd never let him go.

When he finally lifted his mouth from hers, they were both breathless, aching, hot with desire. His eyes dark as midnight, he caught her face in his palms and let his thumb take a slow tour of her just-kissed lips. "Every time I kiss you, I want you more," he murmured roughly. "Let's get out of here."

Slipping his arm around her shoulders, he steered her through the parked vehicles to his truck, his urgency contagious. Her heart beating out a crazy tattoo in her ears, Pru waited impatiently for him to unlock the driver's door, then slid to the middle of the seat, needing to be as close to him as the law and her seat belt would allow. But even with her thigh and hip pressed to his, it wasn't close enough. Until he slipped his arm around her and contentment seeped through her like warm honey, a contentment she'd never known until this man came into her life. This was where she belonged. Where she'd always belonged. Down through time.

He took her back to her apartment, and as he walked her to her door, there was no question that he was coming inside. From the moment he'd slid onto the seat next to her in his truck, he hadn't stopped touching her and he didn't stop now. When she fumbled in her purse for her key, he stood behind her, nuzzling the back of her neck, his own fingers finding her keys as she leaned back against him, her eyes closing on a sigh. One arm wrapped around her waist to hold her close, he unlocked her dead bolt with his free hand, then tugged her inside.

She'd left a light burning, but it did little to dispel the deep, soft shadows that bathed the living room in intimacy. A smile curling up one corner of her mouth, she turned in his arms. "Alone at last."

They needed to talk, but not when the lights were low and his blood was hot for her and the only thing he could think of was just her. Loving her. Pleasing her. Giving himself to her in a way he had no other woman. Taking her hand, he dragged it up to his hammering heart. "I'm staying the night," he rasped.

"Then I guess I won't have to hogtie you to my bed so you can't get away," she teased, brushing a kiss across his mouth. "Darn."

His eyes starting to twinkle, a slow grin spread across his face. "What can I say? I guess I'm just too easy."

"No, this is," she whispered, looping her arms around the strong column of his neck to hold him close while she kissed him. "As easy as falling off a log." Teasing, flirting, her tongue gently seducing, she kissed him in all the ways she'd been dying to for hours. Like the finest wine, the taste of him went to her head, scrambling her thoughts, weakening her knees. Delighted, she leaned into him and hung on for dear life.

Murdock promised himself he was going to take it nice and slow. She deserved nothing less, and for the past two days he'd thought of nothing but how—if he ever got to make love to her again—he was going to make it slow and long and deep. He wanted eons with her, an eternity just to learn where to touch her to make her breath hitch in her throat, where to kiss her to make her groan his name, when to taste her and have her come undone in his arms.

But he wasn't going to be able to manage that tonight. Not when he'd done nothing more than kiss her and he was already hot. Not when he only had to hold her against him to burn with a need that any second threatened to spontaneously combust.

His hands sweeping over her, he tugged impatiently at the buttons of her sweater, murmuring her name in a rough whisper as he tore his mouth from hers to scatter desperate kisses over her face, her throat, the swell of her breasts as her sweater finally parted. God, she was beautiful! How could he have forgotten how beautiful she was?

Not surprised to find his fingers trembling, he reached for her, his knuckles brushing the fullness of her breasts as he unhooked the front clasp of her bra. Then she was free, spilling into his hands, and with a hunger that came from his soul, he suckled at a rosy crest.

Pru strangled a cry that was his name, heat streaking through her like liquid fire. Her knees buckling, she would have fallen at his feet if he hadn't caught her suddenly, his strong arms sweeping her up against his

chest before she could do anything more than gasp.
"Zeb!"

"I've got you, honey," he growled, his longs legs
quickly carrying them down the short length of the hall
to her bedroom. "Just hang on."

She couldn't have let go of him if her life had de-
pended on it. With the sure strides of a man who knew
where he was going, he carried her to her bed without
bothering to turn on a light and gently lowered her to
the down comforter that was as soft as a feather bed. He
would have released her then, but she was having none
of it. Her arms tight around his neck, she pulled him
down on top of her.

"Wait . . ." He choked on a laugh. "My clothes—"

"I'll take care of everything," she promised against
his mouth, pushing him over onto his back.

She was like something out of one of his deepest,
darkest, most erotic fantasies. She moved over him like
a temptress, kissing him as if she couldn't get enough of
him, her eager hands pushing off his shoes, then tugging at his shirt and pants until he was bare and hot and
groaning with need.

Even then, she didn't stop. Murmuring love words,
she trailed kisses down his chest, teased his nipples with
her tongue, made a playful swipe at his navel, making
him burn. But it was the kiss she planted at the top of
his thigh that had him shooting up off the mattress with
a hoarse cry as he reversed their positions and swept her
under him.

In the darkness, his blue eyes glowed like fire down
at her. "You're driving me crazy, honey."

She took that as the highest compliment, her smile
full of mischief as she nipped at his shoulder. "Good.

Because that's how you make me feel. Wild and crazy and so hot I want to melt all over you."

Impossibly moved by her words, he swooped down to take her mouth in a rough kiss, wanting to drown her in pleasure. He soon discovered, it didn't take much to please her. A long, thorough kiss, a nuzzle of her breasts, the slow glide of his hands over her, searching out her secrets. Clinging to him, her breath tearing through her lungs, she moaned, her hips lifting to his.

"Now," she cried hoarsely, wrapping her legs around him. "Love me now."

Another woman he might have been able to resist long enough to drag out the loving until they were both wound tight. But not Pru. Never Pru. He was wild for her before he ever touched her, and it took nothing more than the feel of her legs wrapping around him to drive him straight toward the edge. Her green eyes glowing with a love she made no attempt to hide, she stroked him until he was mindless, her hand incredibly gentle as she guided him home. Groaning, he eased into her and felt her silky sheath close around him, her hips already picking up a rhythm that was uniquely theirs. Entranced, seduced by an intimacy he'd never found with anyone else, and unable to hold back a second longer, he picked up the tempo, groaning as she took him deeper, then deeper still. Until the world faded to black and there was nothing and no one but the two of them racing toward the edge of oblivion. Faster and faster until they tumbled over into the starlight, their mingled cries of pleasure echoing softly all the way to Heaven.

The beard-roughened face that nuzzled her throat the next morning teased at Pru's consciousness, drawing a low moan of pleasure from her. Her eyes still closed, she smiled and stretched like a cat, loving the feel of Zeb's hard, muscled legs tangled with her own and his arms hugging her close. Sated, she could have lain like that for hours and wanted for nothing.

"Mmm. That feels nice," she purred, snuggling deeper into the covers. "What time is it?"

Inhaling the warm, sleepy scent of her, he slowly worked his way up her throat, pressing open-mouthed kisses to skin that was as soft as silk. "A little after nine," he murmured huskily. "Did you sleep well?"

"Mmm-hmm. *Nine!*" she choked, suddenly coming rudely awake. "Ohmygod, I'm late! James is going to have my hide!"

Her heart jumping into overdrive, she bolted up, scrambling out of his arms, only to have him laughingly haul her back down to the mattress and pin her flat on her back under him. "Zeb! What are you doing? Trying to get me fired? Let me up!"

He didn't move so much as a muscle. His dark hair tousled and his chiseled jaw shadowed and unshaven, he grinned down at her crookedly, his blue eyes rueful. "I don't know why I let you get away with calling me that," he grumbled half to himself. "Honey, today's a holiday. We've got the day off."

She remembered then. Veterans Day. How could she have forgotten? Up until he'd appeared on her doorstep last night, she'd been dreading the day off and the empty hours that would give her too much time to think of him.

Her eyes dancing bewitchingly, she draped her arms around his neck. "A whole day off together, hmm? I can't imagine what we're going to do with all that time."

Her stomach chose that moment to growl, reminding them both that neither could remember the last time they'd eaten. "I think I'd better feed you," he said, chuckling, "or you're not going to have the strength to do anything. How 'bout breakfast on the river?"

"Make it O'Toole's and you've got a deal."

At the mention of one of his favorite restaurants on the Riverwalk, he grinned. It never failed to amaze him how much they had in common. If he hadn't known better, he would have sworn she was specially made just for him. "Then it looks like you've got yourself a deal, lady. The last one in the shower picks up the tab."

He was off like a rocket, but she was smaller and quicker and darted into the bathroom two seconds ahead of him. Laughing, they turned into each other's arms under the warm spray and reached for the soap. It was a long time before either of them thought of food again.

They did eventually end up at O'Toole's—after they finally got out of the shower and Zeb had called the site to check with the security guard to make sure everything was all right. It was closer to lunchtime than breakfast and, as usual, the place was packed. One of the most popular spots on the river, the restaurant had outdoor tables right on the edge of the water, lots of plants and dark wood inside, and a live band that really cooked. On Friday nights their seafood buffet was the best in town, and the rest of the time, the menu was no slouch.

Not surprised that Pru had discovered O'Toole's her first week in town—word of mouth brought tourists and locals in by the droves—Murdock draped his arm possessively around her waist and couldn't regret that they had to stand in line for a table. They both knew the food would be worth the wait, and it gave him just that much more time to hold her.

God, she'd nearly burned him alive in that shower. Just thinking about it heated his blood. His arm tightening around her waist, he pulled her closer. When she glanced up at him, her green eyes sultry with promise and reflecting the same memories that were humming deep inside him, it was all he could do not to lower his mouth to hers and make them both forget where they were. Later, he promised himself, and tore his gaze from hers.

The hostess called their name just then, and with Pru's hand tucked into his, they followed her through the maze of tables to one just being cleaned off on the patio. Unseasonably warm for early November, it was a beautiful day to eat outdoors, and it looked like most of San Antonio was taking advantage of it. Not only was the restaurant doing a booming business, the Riverwalk itself was teeming with people. Couples strolling hand in hand eased their way past families with children and strollers, and there were even a few sunbathers lounging in the sunnier spots, soaking up the rays.

Grinning at a set of twins who had ice cream all over themselves and their stroller, Murdock started to point them out to Pru when he suddenly felt someone's watchful gaze on him. Not liking the feeling, he glanced around, only to freeze as his gaze crossed that of two men seated at a table on the other side of the patio. Closer to Pru's age than his own, they didn't appear to be the least concerned that they'd been caught staring. Their eyes shifting from him to Pru and back again, as if they couldn't quite figure out what Pru's relationship was to him. Wife or daughter? Niece or date?

Shrug 'em off, he told himself fiercely. They were just a couple of punks who were still wet behind the ears and didn't know a damn thing about life. If they had, they would have realized he was a far sight from being old and they'd be damn lucky to be in as good a shape as he was when they reached his age. His driver's license might say forty-four, but he didn't feel anywhere close to that and was in better shape now than he had been at twenty.

So who you trying to convince, Murdock? the voice of reason drawled mockingly in his head. *You or yourself?*

His jaw rigid, he stared blindly at his menu, not seeing anything but his own pathetic posturings. He was being too damn sensitive about the difference in their ages, he chided himself furiously. Pru had already made it clear she couldn't care less about numbers. The only significance between her age and his was how long she'd been without him. She loved him.

But would she later? Would she still want him when he was fifty? Sixty? Would she still welcome him into her bed when he was old enough to draw social security benefits and she was still a beautiful young woman in the prime of her life? How would she handle an old man for a lover? And how would he keep up with her?

"What's wrong?"

The quiet question caught him off guard and he glanced up to find her watching him over the top of her menu, her brows knit with worry, the laughter that had skimmed her features only moments before, when she, too, had spotted the ice-cream-covered kids in the stroller, now gone. Her green eyes solemn and her mouth unsmiling, she waited patiently for him to answer.

Forcing a crooked smile, his rueful gaze met hers. "I was just trying to decide if I wanted to try the *fajitas* or not. I've never had them before, but I've heard they'll set your hair on fire. Whaddya say? Want to split an order with me?"

Her eyes searching his, Pru noted the shadows that refused to be dismissed with an easy smile. For the span of a heartbeat she was tempted to press him for the truth about whatever was bothering him, but he obviously didn't want to talk about it. And pressing would only ruin their day together. "I'm game if you are," she said lightly. "Just make sure you order a pitcher of tea, too. I've got a feeling we're going to need it."

He grinned, as she had hoped he would, and whatever was troubling him apparently slipped to the back of his mind. Carefully steering the conversation away from anything serious, she set out to make him laugh out loud, and by the time the food arrived, he was chuckling with her as if he didn't have a care in the world.

As promised, the food was hot, but it wasn't the spices that warmed her from the inside out. It was Zeb. Just having him all to herself, for a whole day, was more than she'd ever dared to hope for. She had only to reach out to touch him, and as they finally left the restaurant an hour later, slipping her hand in his was the most natural thing in the world. And if the shadows she'd seen earlier occasionally drifted through his eyes like clouds across the moon, she tried to tell herself it was just her imagination. He was more relaxed than she'd ever seen him and there couldn't possibly be anything wrong.

They spent the day playing tourist, strolling hand in hand through the shops and art galleries on the river, then wandering over to the Alamo and taking a hushed tour of the chapel just like millions of other sightseers did every year. From there, the zoo beckoned, and the day was too gorgeous for them to resist. Warmed by the springlike sunshine, they fed the bears, laughed at the monkeys, and ate hotdogs as if they hadn't had a bite to eat all day. By the time they left, the sun was just starting to set and they still had the evening ahead of them.

Unable to keep his hands off her, Murdock struggled with the need to take her home with him and spend what was left of the holiday making love to her. They'd been doing a slow mating dance all day, touching, teasing, seducing with a smile, a brush of hips, the anticipation slowly, slowly building until all he could think of was getting her in his bed. But it was early yet and the moment would only be sweeter with the wait.

So he took her back downtown, his hand resting possessively on her knee as she sat thigh to thigh with him in his truck. They could have gone back to the Riverwalk, but it was too crowded there and he wanted her as much to himself as he could manage in a public place. And the best place he could think of was the Tower of Americas.

It was dark and windy on the outdoor observation deck, and they didn't exactly have the place to themselves. But everyone else was looking at the spectacular view of the city at night and he had eyes only for Pru. Murmuring her name, he tugged her into his arms and kissed her in the moonlight.

He knew immediately he'd miscalculated. He wanted her too badly to be satisfied with just a kiss, and she was just as eager as he. Ignoring the kids ten feet away fighting over who got to look through the binoculars next, she raised up on tiptoe, boldly fitted her body to his, her mouth eager under his, her tongue sliding into his mouth where no one could see and rubbing against his, driving him crazy.

The wind whipped away the groan that rose to his throat, while need lodged like a fireball in his gut. His lungs straining for air, he backed her into a corner, intending to take the kiss deeper when his beeper suddenly went off.

"Son of a bitch!" Swearing under his breath, he tore his mouth from hers and grabbed the beeper from his belt, half tempted to throw it over the side of the tower. But one look at the number glowing up at him from the dial and he froze. "It's from the security guard at the site," he said tersely. "C'mon. I've got to find a phone."

They found one outside the tower's revolving restaurant, and as Murdock quickly dialed his office, he braced himself for more bad news. But when Carl Flanders, the ex-marine he'd hired to watch the site at night, came on the line, he hurriedly assured him nothing was wrong. "There was a prowler about thirty minutes ago," he admitted, "but I think it was just a kid looking for mischief and I ran him off."

"Did you call the M.P.'s?"

"Yes, sir. I figured it was better to be safe than sorry, so they went over the place with a fine-tooth comb and came up with absolutely zilch. The place is as quiet as a church now, but I thought you'd want to know what was going on."

The tension easing in his chest, Murdock sighed in relief. "Thanks, Carl, I appreciate that. If anything else happens, don't hesitate to call."

Standing impatiently at his side, Pru asked, "What happened?" as soon as he hung up.

"There was a prowler," he said grimly.

He gave her a quick rundown of the guard's report. "Evidently it was just a kid looking for a cheap thrill. He ran off as soon as he saw Carl, so there's probably nothing to worry about."

"But you are," she guessed shrewdly, studying him with a half smile. He might be as calm as a bank teller giving a customer his balance, but Pru hadn't missed the hard glint in his eyes or the careful way he had hung up the phone, as if he'd just barely resisted slamming it down. He was furious that someone had once again invaded *his* site. "You don't think this was just a kid's prank."

She phrased it as a statement, not a question, and he didn't disagree. "No. Something doesn't feel right."

"Then let's go check it out," she said simply, and pushed the Down button for the elevator.

The site was just as it should have been. The security fence had been repaired and the gates were locked, the floodlights that had been set up at strategic points illuminating every square inch of the compound. Pru took one look at the place and saw how the security guard had spotted a prowler so easily. Nothing could move without being picked up by those lights.

But it was too quiet. Carl Flanders's truck was parked inside the fence, right next to Murdock's office, but he was nowhere in sight. A chill suddenly skating down her spine, Pru shivered. "I don't know how that security guard stays here all night by himself. It's kind of spooky."

"He's got six kids at home," Murdock replied with a quick grin. "This is probably the only place he can get some peace and quiet. Let me tell him we're here and then I want to look around."

With Pru at his side, he unlocked the gates and headed for his office, where he expected to find Carl sitting at his desk, passing the time between his rounds with the stack of crossword puzzles he brought with him every evening to work. But Carl wasn't at his desk. Instead he was passed out cold on the floor with his hands tied behind his back.

"What the hell!" Swearing, Murdock hurried to the older man's side, tossing orders to Pru as he used his pocketknife to cut through the ropes binding Carl's hands. "Call the M.P.'s. And an ambulance. He looks like he took a pretty nasty hit to the side of his head."

Grabbing the phone, Pru hurriedly placed both calls and hung up just as the guard regained consciousness, vicious curses rolling off his tongue as he forced his eyes open. "The bastard came out of nowhere," he groaned, struggling to sit up. "Gotta get him."

"Whoa, man!" Murdock said, gently pushing his shoulders back to the floor. "You're not in shape to catch anyone. You stay right where you are until the ambulance gets here."

"But he might still be here—"

"If he is, I'll catch him—"

"I'm going with you," Pru said quickly. Anticipating an argument, she stuck her chin out, just daring him to try to stop him. "Two pairs of eyes are better than one and this guy has a history of sneaking up on people's blind side. You need me and you don't have time to argue about it."

She was right about that and they knew it. Pinning her with a hard stare, he retrieved his sidearm from his desk and growled, "Stay behind me. And don't do anything stupid. Whoever this idiot is, he means business and I won't have you hurt." Turning his gaze to Carl, he frowned. "Are you sure you'll be okay until the M.P.'s get here?"

"Yes, go... Go!"

Knowing nothing short of hogtying Pru was going to keep her from going with him, Murdock swore and hurried outside with her right behind him. In the silence that shrouded the compound, his whisper hardly carried beyond her ears. "We'll go in through the west wing. If there's any shooting, keep low and find cover. And don't come out till I call you or the M.P.'s get here."

Waiting only for her nod, he rushed across the compound to the west wing with Pru right behind him, as silent as shadows in the night. Slipping through the open doorway, he flattened himself against the wall, his eyes searching the darkness. Only when he was sure there was no one there did he motion for Pru to follow him inside.

Seconds later they made their way through the darkness to the main part of the building. The light was better here, the glare of the floodlights outside spilling through the large windows of the entrance and pushing out the shadows. Quiet as mice, they moved through the rooms, finding nothing.

His guard relaxing slightly, Murdock moved into the east wing, sure the vandal was already gone. Turning to motion Pru into the first office, he didn't see the man busy at work in the shadows across the room until it was too late. Suddenly there was a muttered curse, the flare of a spark, then fire climbing up the wall at the speed of sound. Clearly, defiantly, revealed by the sudden light, Bill Dancer glared back at them.

Pru gasped. No! It couldn't be Bill! He was one of Zeb's best friends. This had to be some terrible mistake. But there was no mistaking the gun he pointed at her and Zeb.

Stunned, Murdock stood at her side, hurt disbelief lodged like a fist in his gut as he stared at his friend as if he'd never seen him before. All this time he'd been looking for a traitor in his midst, he'd never thought to suspect the one man he'd known longer than all of the rest of the crew put together. Why, dammit? Why was he doing this?

"Put the gun away, man, and let's talk about this," he said hoarsely. "Pru, get out of here."

Pru had no intention of leaving him alone with a madman holding a gun, but obviously Bill Dancer didn't know that. "No!" he screamed, and fired.

Ten

_____

The bullet slammed into the wall mere inches from Pru's head. Horrified, she took one look at the hole that could have been in her skull, and suddenly darkness was swamping her brain, sucking her under. For the first time in her life she fainted, sliding bonelessly to the floor.

"Pru!"

His choking cry echoing through the darkness, Murdock launched himself at Bill in a blind rage, but the other man, shocked by his own actions, had already dropped the gun as if it were a grenade that was about to explode in his hand. His arms at his sides, he didn't even try to protect himself when Murdock grabbed him, his fist drawn back to flatten him. But seeing the look of horror on the other man's ashen face as he stared unblinkingly at Pru's crumpled form, Murdock couldn't bring himself to hit him. Not when he stood defenseless in front of him.

Snarling a curse, he released him. "You miserable excuse for a man, if she's hurt, you'd better start saying your prayers." Snatching up the fire extinguisher that had been installed the moment that section of the building had been finished, he put out the fire, then rushed to Pru's side.

"I m-missed her," Bill stuttered. "I—I'm sure of it. I didn't mean to sh-shoot. It just sort of went off."

"Sure it did," Murdock snarled. "And I bet when you snuck up behind me the other night and knocked me out, whatever you hit me with just slipped out of your hand."

"You don't understand. I was desperate."

Unimpressed by his pitiful whine, Murdock gave him a scathing look. "If you thought you were desperate before, just wait till they haul your ass off to jail. Whatever payoff you were getting, I hope it was enough because you're going to need it to hire a good lawyer." Turning his back on him, he reached for Pru's limp hand. "Wake up, honey. It's okay. You're safe now."

His voice calling to her through the fog that clouded her brain made Pru stir, and she opened her eyes abruptly to find Murdock hovering over her in concern. Her heart suddenly slamming, she bolted up, her eyes wide with alarm. "The gun—"

"I've got it," he assured her.

"I don't know what happened, Pru," Bill mumbled. "I—I just lost control...of everything. I lost some money on the horses—"

"You were gambling? That's what all this was about?" Murdock demanded incredulously.

"It wasn't that much," he claimed weakly, wiping his suddenly sweating brow. "But I got behind on the mortgage and Tracy threatened to leave me. I had to do something. So I went to Harold Klawson for a loan—"

Murdock swore. So now they were getting to the nitty-gritty. Harold Klawson wasn't just another builder, he was a force to be reckoned with in the world of government contracts. Hugely successful and rich as Midas, he usually got what he wanted. And he'd wanted the Fort Sam project. He would have gotten it, too...if Murdock hadn't underbid him by a matter of dollars.

"And he just got down on his knees and welcomed you with open arms, didn't he?" he drawled contemptuously. "Knowing Klawson, he probably agreed to give you anything you wanted...for one small little favor in return."

Looking sick, Bill nodded. "It didn't seem so much at the time...just slow things down, sneak back in at night and trash the place up a little. That's all it should have been. But then he wanted you fired—or pressure put on you so you'd quit—and he didn't care how I did it."

"So of course you went along with him."

"It wasn't like that!" he cried. "He'd bought the note on my house. If I didn't do what he said, he was going to toss me out on my ear, and I couldn't let that happen. Tracy would have left me in a heartbeat."

Murdock laughed at that, the harsh sound holding not a trace of amusement. "And you don't think she's going to leave you when you go to federal prison for this? Get real, man. Your butt's fried and you've got no one to blame but yourself."

The wail of sirens cut through the night then, and within minutes paramedics were checking out Carl Flanders in Murdock's office and the M.P.'s had arrived to take Bill into custody. The fire department was called just to make sure that the electrical fire Bill had started didn't flare back up again after everyone had left, and once again, sirens screamed in the night.

Feeling like a fool for fainting, Pru stayed back out of the way, weak-kneed with relief. The nightmare was over. Finally. Lieutenant Barker would notify the San Antonio police of Harold Klawson's role in the plot, and with Bill's signed confession, Klawson, too, would soon be in custody. Then there would be no more ugly surprises for Zeb at the site, no more attacks in the middle of the night. No more threats... for either of them. Zeb would finish the project on time and hopefully under budget, and the men who had tried to destroy him would have a long time behind bars to contemplate the ironies of fate. And it was no more than they deserved.

Watching him confer with Lieutenant Barker, she wanted to cross to him, to walk into his arms and just hold him. Something of her need must have reached out to touch him because suddenly he was looking for her, his narrowed eyes searching the chaos until he found her. With a quick word to the lieutenant, he was striding toward her.

"It looks like I'm going to be here a while," he said with a grimace. "I've got some loose ends to tie up, and I don't know how long it's going to take. Why don't you go on home and I'll drop by later."

She would rather have stayed, but there wasn't anything she could do to help and it had been a long day. If she lived to be a hundred, she didn't think she'd ever forget that bullet slamming into the wall right next to her head. Some time to herself was probably just what she needed. "All right," she said, and only then remembered her car was back at her apartment. "I don't have any wheels."

"Lieutenant Barker said he'd have one of his men take you." Ignoring the interested eyes around them, he caught her chin and lifted her face to the light, not liking her paleness. He could still taste the fear on his tongue from when he'd heard that shot go off and had seen her fall. "Are you sure you'll be all right at your place by yourself? I could probably arrange to have one of the M.P.'s stay until I get there."

It wasn't someone else she wanted, only him. "I'll be fine," she replied huskily, rising on tiptoe to brush a quick, too brief kiss across his mouth. "Stay as long as you need. I'll be waiting for you."

He watched her go, wishing he could call her back, but he had work to do, and if he didn't get on it, he'd be there all night. So with the help of Barker and his men, he went over every inch of the site, taking inventory of the hurried damage Bill had done after he'd knocked out the security guard. Evidently discouraged that he hadn't been able to threaten Murdock into resigning, he'd planned to set electrical fires in every section of the building and burn the place to the ground. If Murdock hadn't arrived when he had, he would have succeeded.

An hour later he was wrapping things up and anxious to get to Pru when Barker approached him with a frown. "I just got a call from the brig. Your friend, Dancer, has been spilling his guts big time ever since he left here. According to him, he wasn't the only one Klawson paid off to give you grief. You ever heard of a big shot in the inspector's office by the name of Bruce James?"

"Hell, yes," he retorted, surprised. "That's Pru's boss."

"Well, if you've been having problems with the inspector's office, you can blame him. He was taking a nice tidy sum to hold up production every chance he got. Evidently, the inspectors he sent over here were under strict orders to be as picky as hell. Dancer said that's why Pru was reassigned. James was afraid she was getting too chummy with you and he couldn't trust her to do the job the way he wanted it done."

"Son of a bitch," Murdock swore. "I never met the bastard, but he gave Pru nothing but hell. Has he been arrested, yet?"

Barker grinned. "He and Klawson are already on their way downtown with a couple of San Antonio's finest. Don't you just love a happy ending?"

Murdock laughed for the first time in what seemed like hours, relief snapping the tension that had gripped him by the back of the neck ever since he and Pru had arrived to find the security guard out cold on his office floor. "Thanks for the update," he said, slapping the other man on his shoulder. "You don't know what a load that is off my mind. Thanks, man."

"Anytime," Barker said. "So now that the rats are all rounded up, why don't you go ahead and get out of here? There's nothing more you can do and we'll lock up when we leave."

It was a suggestion that he didn't have to make twice. Within minutes, Murdock was in his truck and headed for Pru's, his thoughts automatically skipping ahead to her. The past twenty-four hours he'd spent with her had been precious moments stolen out of time, a dream that bordered on fantasy, an illusion that couldn't last. He'd known that, but he hadn't been able to resist pretending, just for a little while, that they were like any other lovers who didn't have a care in the world. But reality had intruded and it was time for him to face the music.

He was crazy in love with her, probably had been from the moment he'd laid eyes on her. But love wasn't a magic potion that made everything all right. It couldn't take away the years that he'd already lived before she was even born. It couldn't change how people would look at them when they saw a sweet young thing with an old man.

She was going to fight him on this—he knew that as well as he knew he'd go to his grave loving her, missing her—but he'd made up his mind. He loved her too much to saddle her with an old man for the rest of her life, and nothing she could say was going to change that.

His thoughts on her and not on his driving, he was halfway to her house when he suddenly noticed the fog. It came out of nowhere, rolling out of the darkness like a tidal wave, engulfing him in thick, swirling clouds that immediately blocked out the rest of the world. Muttering a curse, he immediately let up off the accelerator, but it was too late. With frightening speed, he raced into a wall of vapor so dense that he could only see a couple of feet in front of the nose of his truck.

His heart thumping, he slowed to a crawl, the twin beams of his headlights hardly penetrating the soupy mixture. He could hardly see the center stripe and doubted that anyone else on the road could, either. Knowing he should pull over but wanting to get to Pru's, he tightened his grip on the steering wheel and drove on.

He never saw the old man step out in front of him. One minute there was nothing in the road but the fog, and the next he was bearing down on a skinny wisp of a man who had to be eighty if he was a day.

"Son of a—" Swearing, Murdock slammed on the brakes, but the road was wet and he started to skid. Unable to do anything, he watched in horror as his truck finally shuddered to a stop with the old fellow right in front of his wheels.

Terrified he'd hurt him, Murdock was out of his pickup like a shot, sure he hadn't hit the man but afraid he might have scared him into a heart attack. Rushing up to him, he demanded, "Are you all right? God, I didn't even see you! Here, let me find you a place to sit. You look a little shaky."

If the old gentleman heard him, he gave no sign of it. "A mistake," he mumbled, looking around as if he were lost and hadn't even seen the truck that had almost flattened him. "How could I have made such a mistake?"

Murdock frowned. "Are you lost? Can I take you somewhere?"

"I walked away from the best thing that ever happened to me just because it didn't come in the package I expected. I was so stupid!" He shook his head in bewilderment. "I didn't think—"

Agitated, he glanced up at Murdock suddenly, as if he'd known he was there all the time, and grabbed him by the arm with a fierceness that was surprising for a man his age. "Don't do it!" he said hoarsely. "Don't make the same mistake I did."

"No, I won't," Murdock tried to assure him in a calm, soothing voice. "Now, why don't you just sit—"

"Promise me," the old man cut in desperately. "Don't question a gift life throws in your path. Treasure it. Even if it's only for an hour, a month, it can bring you the kind of happiness that will make up for a lifetime of loneliness. You must believe me!" he pleaded. "I know what I'm talking about."

A rising note of hysteria nearly choked him, but it was the wild look in the old gent's eyes that scared the hell out of Murdock. Afraid he was going to have a stroke or something, he tried to soothe him even as he untangled himself from his biting grip. "I believe you," he assured him. "There's no need for you to get all upset about this. I'm not stupid enough to turn my back on a gift. Here, sit down while I get a blanket out of my truck. I'll be right back."

As good as his word, he only took thirty seconds to sprint back to his truck and grab the old army blanket he kept stashed behind the seat. "It's damn cold out tonight," he said as he hurried back to the front of his truck. "I don't know where this fog came from, but this should warm you up pretty good—"

The blanket gripped tight in his hand, he stopped in his tracks and stared in disbelief at the spot where he'd left the old man. He was gone.

"Son of a—" Confused, he looked around wildly, afraid the old gentleman had wandered off the side of the road into the fog and possibly collapsed somewhere. The night wasn't predicted to be that cold, but the dampness couldn't be good for old bones or fragile lungs, and he couldn't just leave him.

Murdock worriedly searched nearly a block in every direction, sure that the man hadn't had time to take more than a dozen steps at the most. But there was no sign of him anywhere. He'd literally vanished into thin air.

I'm losing it, Murdock thought shakily. He had to be. Either that or he'd somehow stepped into an old episode of the "Twilight Zone." Maybe he needed a vacation, he decided, a few days off from work to get away for a while so he could just vegetate . . . before the men in white coats came to haul him away.

Frowning, he returned to his truck and climbed in, tossing the blanket down on the seat. He couldn't spend the whole night looking for an old man who obviously didn't want to be found. Pru was waiting for him and had probably already fallen asleep.

Half expecting the old man to step back out in front of him at any second, he slowly continued toward Pru's, but he didn't see a living soul. Only the fog that swirled around him, surrounding him, cutting him off from the rest of the world so effectively that there wasn't even a light or road sign to give him his bearings.

I walked away from the best thing that ever happened to me just because it didn't come in the package I expected.

The old man's words rang in his ears, taunting him, haunting him, refusing to be ignored until he suddenly, *finally* heard them. Dear God, was that what he was doing? Preparing to walk away from the only woman he'd ever loved because whenever he'd thought about spending his life with someone, he'd just assumed she'd be as old as he was? Where was it carved in stone that they had to be anywhere near the same age?

Don't question a gift life throws in your path. Treasure it. Even if it only lasts for an hour, a month, it can bring you the kind of happiness that will make up for a lifetime of loneliness.

Hitting the steering wheel with the palm of his hand, he spit out a short, pithy oath. God, what a fool he'd been! If he hadn't been so disgusted with himself, he would have laughed at his own blindness. He'd been so hung up on the difference in their ages and the things they couldn't possibly have in common because of that, that he hadn't been using his head for anything but a resting place for his hard hat. So what if he was going to be forty-five? He came from a long line of good, sturdy stock. The men in the family had a history of living to at least ninety and the women even longer than that.

Which meant, if they were lucky, that he and Pru could have at least forty-five years together, which was more than could be said of most couples. And if they weren't blessed with that kind of time, then the old man was right. Knowing she was his forever, having her at his side and in his bed—for whatever length of time they were fated to have—would more than make up for all the years without her.

Shaken by how close he'd actually come to making the biggest mistake of his life, his foot flattened on the accelerator to send his truck surging forward, the sudden need to get to her a hundred times stronger than the need for caution in the fog. But between one heartbeat and the next, the mist lifted as quickly as it had fallen, giving him a clear view of the road that led as straight as an arrow to Pru's apartment. Seeing clearly for the first time since he'd looked down into a pair of flashing green eyes and known his fate was sealed, he laughed and raced, unchecked, toward his destiny.

Too restless to sit still, Pru paced over to the front windows of her apartment and parted the curtains to gaze out at the parking lot. Nothing had changed since she'd checked five minutes ago, then five minutes before that. There wasn't a sign of Murdock's truck anywhere.

Turning away, she cursed softly under her breath. Where *was* he? Something was wrong. It had to be or he would have been here by now, she told herself worriedly. Unless he'd decided not to stop by after all.

Even before the thought was fully formed, she rejected it. He wouldn't do that to her, not after last night and the loving they'd shared. Not after today, when he'd kept her hand in his most of the day. Not after tonight, when he'd nearly taken Bill apart when he'd come too close to shooting her. No, something was wrong. Maybe she should call the base...

The knock at the door caught her halfway to the phone and nearly weakened her knees. "Thank God!" she breathed, jerking open the door to him. "I've been worried sick. What took so long?"

Needing to hold her, he stepped inside and shut the door, reaching for her in one smooth motion to haul her against him. "You wouldn't believe it," he said, wrapping her close. "I nearly hit an old man—"

"What!" Startled, she drew back far enough to see his face. "How? What happened? Was he hurt?"

"No, only God knows how." Still baffled, he gave her a brief accounting of the bizarre episode as he sank down to the couch with her. "It was the craziest thing," he said, frowning as he finished the tale. "I couldn't have turned my back for a couple of seconds to get that blanket, but when I turned back, the old guy was gone. Poof. Just like that—" he snapped his fingers "—into the fog."

Puzzled, Pru frowned. "What fog? There wasn't any fog tonight."

"Sure there was. It was thick as pea soup until a couple of minutes ago. You must have seen it if you came home through the park."

Since cutting through Olmos Park was the shortest and most direct route from the base to her apartment, she always went home that way. "There was no fog, Zeb," she said quietly. "In the park or anywhere between here and the base. It was clear as a bell."

His brows knit in puzzlement, he stared down at her, searching for the teasing glint in her eyes. But they were dead serious, her mouth unsmiling. She wasn't kidding—she hadn't seen the fog. And there was no way a mist that thick could have formed in the short time be-

tween when she'd left the base and when he had followed her. Which meant he had either imagined the
whole thing, which he was sure he hadn't, or someone
had been trying to tell him something and he'd had to
practically run over the message before it had pene-
trated the fog in his brain.

Too close, he thought, floored by his own blindness.
He'd come too damn close to losing her. Taking her
hand, he twined his fingers with hers and held on tight.
"I can't explain what happened in the park, honey. All
I know is that old man got me thinking and I thank God
he did."

Her heart started to thump at the heat in his eyes, and
Pru swallowed. "How? What did he say to you?"

He told her, his voice growing gruffer with every
word. "After I talked to him, I realized I was worrying
about so many stupid things...like how young you were
and how old I am, and how there couldn't possibly be
a future for us when there were so many years between
us."

Her heart in her eyes, Pru could only cling to his
hand. "Are you saying those things don't matter anymore?"

"I love you," he said simply, huskily, and was
stunned at how easy it was to say the words. It felt like
he'd been waiting forever just to tell her. Suddenly
feeling impossibly free, he laughed and hauled her into
his lap, crushing her close. "I love you!" Why had it
taken him so long to see it? To admit it? "Do you hear
me, woman?" he growled, scattering kisses across her
face. "I'm nuts about you. Certifiably crazy over you.
Say you'll marry me. Say it," he urged thickly, giving
her a long, hungry kiss. "I need to hear the words."

Pru didn't hesitate; she didn't even have to think.
She'd been born to hear those words from this man.

"I'll marry you," she whispered, her green eyes glistening with tears, her lips trembling with a smile she couldn't contain. "Tonight, tomorrow, just as soon as we can find a preacher."

Delighted, a crooked grin flirted with the corners of his mouth. "What's the matter?" he teased, tightening his arms around her. "You afraid I'll change my mind?"

"Not a chance," she purred, her smile turning sultry as she pressed a quick kiss to the pulse thundering at the base of his throat. "You're mine, Zeb Murdock, and don't you forget it."

"Never," he promised hoarsely, burying his hands in her hair to tilt her face up to his. "I don't know how much time we've got, honey. I guess no one does. I just know I want to spend it with you."

Tears of happiness spilling over her lashes, Pru gazed into the dark blue, loving depths of his wonderful eyes and saw all her dreams coming true. "We can have forever," she whispered, kissing him. "Trust me. I know what I'm talking about."

Epilogue

The church was packed with well-wishers, every pew filled as the organist started the "Wedding March." Unconcerned with the lack of seating, the crowd of angels floating unseen above the heads of the guests immediately lifted their voices in a joyous song of everlasting love that echoed all the way to the walls of Heaven. Pleased, St. Peter even hummed along, his affectionate gaze trained unwaveringly on his two favorite souls as they came together and joined hands in front of their friends and family and before the minister, their love light so strong it set the church and every heart in it aglow.

At his mentor's side, Joshua was so excited he almost floated right up through the vaulted ceiling. "This is so wonderful, sir! I know you were confident that they would find each other, but even you must admit that things looked a little shaky when Zebadiah planned to break things off with Prudence after he caught his friend trying to burn down the construction site. If that fog hadn't rolled in and that old man hadn't stepped in front of his truck, things would have been vastly different."

St. Peter merely smiled and wisely observed, "I never leave the important things to chance, Joshua. Sometimes even a good man with the best of intentions makes a wrong decision and needs a helping hand to get back on the right path."

Stunned, Joshua gasped. "You mean, that was *you,* sir? But I didn't think you were allowed to materialize in the physical realm."

Amused, St. Peter fairly shimmered with good humor. "When you have the ear of the right—person, shall we say?—nothing is impossible. Especially when it comes to love. When it's the kind that's meant to be, it can move Heaven and Earth."

"Oh, I know, sir," Joshua said happily. "Watching Prudence and Zebadiah find each other has been the most rewarding experience. I just don't know what I'm going to do with myself now that they're together."

"Try watching 'All My Children,'" St. Peter suggested. "I understand Erica is in trouble again. Shh, now. They're coming to the good part. Listen."

I, Prudence, take thee. Zebadiah, to have and to hold, from this day forward, for better, for worse, for richer, for poorer, in sickness and in health, until death do us part.

"And even then," St. Peter said softly. "Even then."

"Amen," an even stronger voice added from above, setting the air of the church humming with love. *"Good job, Peter. I especially liked the fog."*

Grinning, Peter practically beamed. "Thank you, Sir. I thought you would."

"You can't rest on your laurels, though, you know. There's a lot more work to be done. In fact, I've been meaning to talk to you about a couple in New York..."

* * * * *

SILHOUETTE®

Desire®

1995

Don't let the winter months get you down because the heat is about to get turned way up...with the sexiest hunks of 1995!

January: *A NUISANCE*
by Lass Small

February: *COWBOYS DON'T CRY*
by Anne McAllister

March: *THAT BURKE MAN*
the 75th Man of the Month
by Diana Palmer

April: *MR. EASY*
by Cait London

May: *MYSTERIOUS MOUNTAIN MAN*
by Annette Broadrick

June: *SINGLE DAD*
by Jennifer Greene

MAN OF THE MONTH...
ONLY FROM
SIILHOUETTE DESIRE

MOM95JJ-R

SILHOUETTE®

Desire

A new series from Nancy Martin

Who says opposites don't attract?

Three sexy bachelors
should've seen trouble coming
when each meets a woman
who makes his blood boil—
and not just because she's beautiful....

In March—
THE PAUPER AND THE PREGNANT PRINCESS (#916)

In May—
THE COP AND THE CHORUS GIRL (#927)

In September—
THE COWBOY AND THE CALENDAR GIRL

Watch the sparks fly as these handsome hunks fall for
the women they swore they didn't want!
Only from Silhouette Desire.

ANNOUNCING THE

FLYAWAY VACATION SWEEPSTAKES!

This month's destination:

Beautiful SAN FRANCISCO!

This month, as a special surprise, we're offering an exciting FREE VACATION!

Think how much fun it would be to visit San Francisco "on us"! You could ride cable cars, visit Chinatown, see the Golden Gate Bridge and dine in some of the finest restaurants in America!

The facing page contains two Entry Coupons (as does every book you received this shipment). Complete and return *all* the entry coupons; **the more times you enter, the better your chances of winning!**

Then keep your fingers crossed, because you'll find out by June 15, 1995 if you're the winner! If you are, here's what you'll get:

- Round-trip airfare for two to beautiful San Francisco!
- 4 days/3 nights at a first-class hotel!
- $500.00 pocket money for meals and sightseeing!

Remember: The more times you enter, the better your chances of winning!*

*NO PURCHASE OR OBLIGATION TO CONTINUE BEING A SUBSCRIBER NECESSARY TO ENTER. SEE REVERSE SIDE OR ANY ENTRY COUPON FOR ALTERNATIVE MEANS OF ENTRY.

VSF KAL

FLYAWAY VACATION
SWEEPSTAKES

OFFICIAL ENTRY COUPON

This entry must be received by: MAY 30, 1995
This month's winner will be notified by: JUNE 15, 1995
Trip must be taken between: JULY 30, 1995-JULY 30, 1996

YES, I want to win the San Francisco vacation for two. I understand the prize includes round-trip airfare, first-class hotel and $500.00 spending money. Please let me know if I'm the winner!

Name_____

Address _____ Apt. _____

City   State/Prov.   Zip/Postal Code

Account #_____

Return entry with invoice in reply envelope.

© 1995 HARLEQUIN ENTERPRISES LTD.   CSF KAL

FLYAWAY VACATION
SWEEPSTAKES

OFFICIAL ENTRY COUPON

This entry must be received by: MAY 30, 1995
This month's winner will be notified by: JUNE 15, 1995
Trip must be taken between: JULY 30, 1995-JULY 30, 1996

YES, I want to win the San Francisco vacation for two. I understand the prize includes round-trip airfare, first-class hotel and $500.00 spending money. Please let me know if I'm the winner!

Name_____

Address _____ Apt. _____

City   State/Prov.   Zip/Postal Code

Account #_____

Return entry with invoice in reply envelope.

© 1995 HARLEQUIN ENTERPRISES LTD.   CSF KAL